ENCHANTED TALES

Edited By Megan Roberts

First published in Great Britain in 2020 by:

Young Writers
Remus House
Coltsfoot Drive
Peterborough
PE2 9BF
Telephone: 01733 890066
Website: www.youngwriters.co.uk

Printed and bound in the UK by BookPrintingUK
Website: www.bookprintinguk.com
YB0438U

FOREWORD

Welcome, Reader!

Are you ready to enter the Adventure Zone? Then come right this way - your portal to endless new worlds awaits. It's very simple, all you have to do is turn the page and you'll be transported into a wealth of super stories.

Is it magic? Is it a trick? No! It's all down to the skill and imagination of primary school pupils from around the country. We gave them the task of writing a story on any topic, and to do it in just 100 words! I think you'll agree they've achieved that brilliantly – this book is jam-packed with exciting and thrilling tales.

These young authors have brought their ideas to life using only their words. This is the power of creativity and it gives us life too! Here at Young Writers we want to pass our love of the written word onto the next generation and what better way to do that than to celebrate their writing by publishing it in a book!

It sets their work free from homework books and notepads and puts it where it deserves to be – out in the world and preserved forever. Each awesome author in this book should be **super proud** of themselves, and now they've got proof of their ideas and their creativity in black and white, to look back on in years to come!

We hope you enjoy this book as much as we have. Now it's time to let imagination take control, so read on...

CONTENTS

Roza Daif (9) 52
Maryam Gitey (8) 53
Gabriel Selimi (8) 54
Maraam Bashraheel (8) 55

Hareleeshill Primary School, Larkhall

Matheus Caoile (11) 56
John Mooney (12) 57
Tyler McCallum (11) 58
Abi Douglas (11) 59
Jack Dingwall (11) 60
Lennox McLear (11) 61
Tilly Lindsay (11) 62
Brooke Kane (11) 63

Haughton St Giles CE Primary Academy, Haughton

Arabella Violet Mai Hughes (10) 64
Jack George Marsh (9) 65
Leah Costley (8) 66
Emelia Allen (7) 67
Beatrice Rose Palmer (9) 68
Henry Timmis (10) 69
Harry Marsh (7) 70

Kessingland CE Primary Academy, Kessingland

Matthew Pope-Brannon (9) 71
Daisy Jackson (9) 72
Billy Willis (10) 73
Lewis Wilson Burgess (10) 74
Lacey Brookman (9) 75
Laila Young (10) 76
Maddox Larter (10) 77
Hollie Mary Grace Chambers (9) 78

North Walsall Primary Academy, Walsall

Malika Qurban (8) 79
Evie Weseley (9) 80
Eliza Akhtar (9) 81
Naomi Smith (9) 82
Habibah Bibi (8) 83

Oakwood Primary School, Glasgow

Jack Thomas Boyce (10) 84
Ellie Longridge (10) 85
Karra Norman (10) 86
Kaisey-Lee Rae (9) 87
Lucy Rooney (10) 88
Lewis McKenzie (9) 89
Lucy Thomson (10) 90
Chantelle Catherine Blyth (10) 91
Junior Allan (10) 92
Owen White (10) 93
Amy Collins (10) 94
Kayleigh Duncan (10) 95
Casey Etherson (10) 96
Oliwia Kurowska (10) 97

Rockbeare CE Primary School, Rockbeare

Mia Priddis (10) 98
Evangeline Exell (9) 99
Ruby Curran (10) 100
Temperance F (10) 101
Charlie Moore (10) 102
Amy Bourne (11) 103
Connor Davey (10) 104

Rossington St Michael's CE Primary School, Old Rossington

Daisy Taylor (9) 105
Constance Rose-Tottie (9) 106
Jessica Littlewood (10) 107
Victoria Karolina Mirga (9) 108

Rushbury CE Primary School, Rushbury

Evie Medlicott (11)	109
Edward Noblet (8)	110
Freya Bromley (8)	111
Katie Northwood (7)	112
Isabella Whale (8)	113
Darcey Jayne Blackwell (7)	114
Eleanor Merrill (8)	115
Josie Wilson (11)	116
Isabel Frost (9)	117
Hannah Price (7)	118
Ryleigh-Mae Young (10)	119
Isla Grace Hercock (7)	120
Isaac Stokes (7)	121

St John's Priory School, Banbury

Dan Martin (9)	122
Evangelie Fisher (8)	123
Klara Jamrozinska (8)	124
Maya Rose McManus (8)	125

St Joseph's Catholic Primary School, Hertford

Noah Couldridge (9)	126
Shay Lawlor (9)	127
Lilian Lunness (9)	128
Edison Murray (10)	129
Harry Serjeant (9)	130
Gabriella Hunte (10)	131

St Margaret's At Hasbury CE Primary School, Hasbury

Ruby Jane Skett (10)	132
William Dennis Fairclough (10)	133
Zahra Gul (11)	134
Mohammed Ibrahim Hussain (10)	135
Alyssa Marie Bodin (10)	136
Malak Salih (9)	137
Anais Olivia Palmer (9)	138

Molly Varney (9)	139
Molly-Mae Priest (10)	140
Zachary Joe Eeles (9)	141
Phoebe Whitehouse (10)	142

St Mark's CE Primary School, Tunbridge Wells

Chloe Godman (8)	143
Emma Lukowska (8)	144
Asya Celik (8)	145
Idthel Kaniyara (9)	146
Brooke Simmons (10)	147
Rosie Jane Layberry (10)	148
Aimee Kirkness King (10)	149
Harley Squires (10)	150
Dylan Squires (7)	151
Alfie Wright (10)	152
Tyler Sturmer (9)	153
Nyah Leek (8)	154
Pixie Lewis (8)	155
Aimee Leigh Watson (11)	156
Valentina Stopps (11)	157
Emily Lewis (9)	158
Alfie Abrosimoff Jubb (10)	159

Tudor Grange Samworth Academy, Leicester

Isabella Patricia Patterson (11)	160
Charlotte Garratt (10)	161
Leo Crawford (10)	162
Thomas Piotr Stepien (10)	163
Ivana Golic (11)	164
Ella Rudkin (11)	165
Kaisha Nugent (10)	166
Ruby Tebbutt (11)	167
Fia Fragnoli (10)	168
Shaan Hussain (10)	169
Peace Omorogieva (10)	170
Divine Mushinga (10)	171
Arjunpal Singh (10)	172

Yattendon School, Horley

Freya Hawley (8)	173
Affan Saymum (8)	174
Kirsty JJ Writer (10)	175
Isabella Valentina Carvajal Chacin (10)	176
Mohammad Islam (7)	177
Lucas Griffin (8)	178
Ruby Westwood (8)	179
Phoebe May Bellinger (8)	180
Olivia Harding (9)	181

Yealand CE Primary School, Yealand Redmayne

Maisie Elizabeth Thompson (10)	182
James Proctor (11)	183
Luke Zak Robinson (10)	184
Ellie Proctor (11)	185
Sebastian Bould (10)	186
Max Ideson (10)	187

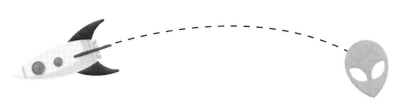

THE STORIES

TOP SECRET

The Ship, The Alien And The Black Hole

The titanium silver spaceship zoomed through space. Their goal was a deadly black hole. The fuel was alright. The engine worked calmly. They came to the goal. They found ATS350 which was 3,000,000 light years away! The crew solaced as they noticed, however, something followed them. A group of peculiar-looking creatures with antennae. They ate asteroids and meteoroids and had humans for a treat. Unexpectedly, the siren went on. "Evacuate!" shouted the captain immediately. Slowly the ship became vacant. The aliens clambered on. Finally, the captain evacuated. This meant something. They passed the mission and found knowledge about aliens!

Safwan Mahfuz (9)
Bonner Primary School, Mile End

Volcano Land

I stepped into the volcano land, not knowing where I would stay. "Ted, look at that!" I said.
"Wow!" he replied.
We saw two green small baby dinos all alone in the dark wilderness. "We should help them, after all they're babies!" I exclaimed.
"True," he said. "Argh!" he screamed.
"Calm down!" I shouted.
We heard sizzling and rumbling. "What's that?" I whispered.
Clash! Lava spilt out of the old, rusty volcano. "All the dinos and dragons, I summon you to help stop the explosion!" I shouted. We stopped the explosion together. Then we all went home.

Amelia Lisa Patricia Smith (10)
Bonner Primary School, Mile End

Through The Portal

As Alice cautiously stepped through the portal, she actually slipped on a screwdriver! She was so confused. Why were there scientists busily rushing back and forth in front of her? She turned back to the portal but, to her surprise, it had vanished! In its place was a giant, gold rocket. She drew nearer and noticed it said *Comet 3*. In the distance, she squinted and spotted a small dot on the horizon. "It's time for lift-off!" announced the dot, staring at the blue, cloudy sky soon to be a pitch-black universe littered with gleaming stars...

Ivy Edith Tighe (9)
Bonner Primary School, Mile End

Twilight

Once upon a time, there was a glamourous shiny unicorn, its name was Twilight. Twilight liked bright colours and stars, she was an extremely playful unicorn and loved to play with her unicorn friends and loved magic because she thought it was satisfying. She loved the smell of lavender. She really loved rainbows and the colours on the rainbow. Twilight lived in a house made out of clouds, rainbow and magic. Twilight was up for anything. She was proud of what she was and had done. Her personality was happy and she was always in a good mood.

Asanti Ahmed (10)
Bonner Primary School, Mile End

Blobby Bob Saves The World Of Blackcurrant

Once there was a hero called Blobby. Blobby was hungry so he went to McDonald's and he saw a villain called Megablob. Megablob stole a woman's purse! Blobby saw what happened and chased him across the sky. Megablob was tired. Blobby saw Megablob faint. He got out the smelliest fart spray in the world and sprayed it on Megablob. He then heard the crowd cheer. Megablob was arrested and a woman beat him up. Megablob cried. The cheering crowd laughed. Blobby was the best alien hero in the world of Blackcurrant. He was a true hero!

Imani Ahmed (9)
Bonner Primary School, Mile End

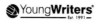
The Case Of The Missing Mince Pies!

Agent Mince had a case to solve: who took the mince pies? It might seem little, but it was very serious. First, he checked the clues. There were crumbs everywhere. Who was a messy eater? He checked the cookie-maker who said, "I don't even eat mince pies!" innocently. He was quite convincing. Same with the baker and the judge. The prime minister wasn't very convincing. "Wait! it could've been mice, thieving little mice. They live in the bin so they need food!" said Agent Mince. He looked and found out that he was right!

Jacob Milne (9)
Bonner Primary School, Mile End

The Letter

Violet was eating breakfast when her mum called her sister to get the post. There was a roll of parchment for Violet so she opened it. She gasped as it said it was from Lexy Castle to inform her that she was a witch! In the letter it said she needed three spellbooks and Standard Grade Of Spells. She also needed a broomstick, a cauldron, uniform, an owl and a hat. She read where to meet: 'At Platform 9 3/4 at Waterloo Station'. She needed to buy her things at Poppey Alley. She couldn't believe she was a witch!

Mia Zheng (9)
Bonner Primary School, Mile End

Zoom!

There once was a girl who got to go to the moon. It was 'take your kid to work day' and Nadia's dad worked for NASA. Suddenly, there was a rush of people and Nadia got pushed. "Ow!" Nadia groaned. As she got up, she realised she was in a space shuttle. Then the whole building shook and she was thrust into darkness! Nadia felt petrified. She realised that she was in space! Nadia excitedly grabbed a spacesuit and joyfully leapt outside. She laughed as she was the first person to stand tall on the famous moon!

Laila Jamil (9)
Bonner Primary School, Mile End

No Books Allowed In Land

I went to the beach to see if there were any books to destroy with my superpowers. When I arrived at the beach, I was suddenly shocked at how many people were reading books. I got really mad and asked myself why people even read books. I immediately got my laser gun out and started to shoot the books. You wouldn't believe how many books I had to destroy!

At last, every book in the world was destroyed and, when I went home, I started to celebrate with my family. My family was happy to see me.

Mehrin Jalil (9)
Bonner Primary School, Mile End

Saving Dinosaurs

One night, there was a superhero called Jack and an evil person called Bob. Bob was going to rule the Earth so he went to his base. He planned to send a huge red meteorite even though he hated balls.

A few weeks later, the superhero (Jack) found out. The meteorite was just about ready to wipe out all the dinosaurs. In a few days' time, the superhero with his red fancy cape used all his strength as it went towards Earth. Jack pushed it so hard with his force that it went to another planet!

Safwan Talha Hassan (9)

Bonner Primary School, Mile End

Bolt Blast

As Jake saw a bright star, he gazed at it for some time but the star turned out to be a bolt! When it hit the house, Jake saw stars and he ran to the city at peculiar speeds. He ran so fast, he bumped into somebody but that person was stealing a watch and it threw him. Jake then caught him and threw the man in jail. The army gave Jake an award and a superhero suit like Superman's but better. It was made of vibranium. They said, "Who are you?" Jake said, "Volt Blast!"

Malakye Jordan Meeko (10)
Bonner Primary School, Mile End

Great Escape

What was I meant to do? Suddenly, I heard a noise. The bars slid right off my window! Ron was in the driver's seat. I got my wand, broom and robes. I was about to get in but my mother grasped my ankle. Together, we tugged my leg until it was free. Soon we were soaring in the sky. In the distance, the sun was setting. Birds tweeted happily as we passed them. It had been days since I'd left the house. I was as free as the birds. Finally, I was free! I was very, very happy.

Aurony Prodhan (10)
Bonner Primary School, Mile End

The Sugarplum Fairy

Sophie sat on her bed looking distraught. How could her mother leave her? How could her kind, loving mother leave her with her horrible father? "Crying again, Miss Sophie?" asked her maid. It was only when the old cow left that Sophie heard a tinkle. "Who's there?" she called, her head snapping around. *Must be my imagination,* she thought. Then there was a tap on her shoulder. "Sophie, is it? Cheer up, it's not like the world's ended." It was a tiny voice and, as Sophie now knew, it was a fairy. "Here, let me take you to my world..."

Josephine R Newman (10)
Brownmead Academy, Shard End

In The Year 3000

The crash site shone with fiery glows and embers flying through the still, dull air. The object flashed and the sliding door swung open, sending smoke into the hemisphere. Inside the ship was a gateway held open by sea-blue chains. Inside the gateway flowed a purple liquid swirling inside it, flourishing and rippling. Stupidly, I ran straight into the liquid. As I entered, I felt my body change and return back to normal. As my eyes adjusted, I saw gigantic ash and smoke clouds smothering the blue sky. I realised this was the future where we polluted Earth.

Billy Mark Brown (10)
Brownmead Academy, Shard End

The Journey

Going into space, adrenaline running through my body. Stepping on the rough craters, every bounce taking me by surprise. I made it. Success filled my mind, but I carried on. Months of planning, years of dreaming. I achieved the unachievable. I'd made it. For the next two years, this was my home.
On September 4th 3200, I witnessed a hole in the sky. It shone as brightly as the morning sun. It was almost... welcoming. I approached it. I put my hand out, reaching for it. At that moment, I realised I'd made a massive mistake. What had I done...?

Samuel Wright (10)

Brownmead Academy, Shard End

Christmas Worries

It was November 30th, everybody was ready for Christmas. The only thing was Julie's missing Elf on the Shelf. Julie tried everything to get her elf Tickles back. Unfortunately, nothing worked. Julie woke up on December 1st, rushed downstairs to see if Tickles had come back, but he hadn't. As the day went on, Julie noticed something peculiar on the Christmas tree. She ran upstairs to tell her mom that something wasn't right, so they both went downstairs and something very magical had happened: Tickles was back!

Holly Parfitt (10)
Brownmead Academy, Shard End

The Moon Rabbit

The long wet grass soaked my bare legs. Crickets buzzed and the wind howled. I saw a shiny red apple reflecting the moonlight and glinting from a creaky tree. As I walked over, everything fell deathly silent. The moon was covered by clouds and I heard scurrying in the distance. I looked up and saw a silhouette on the moon. It had two long ears and was the size of a ferret. Remembering the apple, I dashed towards the tree. I slipped on some mud and fell. I was so scared, I knew it could only be the Moon Rabbit...

Paige Wilson (11)
Brownmead Academy, Shard End

Hide-And-Seek!

One dark afternoon, Jeremy and his friends went to a haunted house to play hide-and-seek. Jeremy said he would seek first. Everyone went to hide. He heard lots of creaks from above. "Three, two, one, ready or not, here I come!" Jeremy set off.

Five minutes later, he heard a scream, one after another. He couldn't find anyone so he shouted, "I give up!" Usually, when he gave up, the people who were hiding would come out and come to him, but no one came so he set off to look. On the floor, he saw blood...

Louis McCaffery (10)
Brownmead Academy, Shard End

The Sword Of Truth!

It was a misty day and Jim, Jet and Jimmy had just found the mansion of secrets. They had just creaked the door open and, *whoosh!* they fell into a pit of doom. There was a huge snake that had a sword for a tail. Could it be the sword of truth? No, it had no ruby on its centre. Jimmy suddenly transformed into a wolf and attacked. The sword immediately fell off and got stuck inside the bricks and fell through. *Crash!* A wall fell over and there it was, the sword of truth before their eyes...

Kayden Leon King (11)
Brownmead Academy, Shard End

A Glowing Nightmare

The NASA rocket was launched. "We're now in space, Clair!"
"I can see Earth!"
Two weeks later, they had just landed on Mars and they started to explore the tiny planet. Jamie and Clair went one way and Dave went the other. Dave found a cave, he saw something glowing. He stepped further into the cave and it killed him. The creature went to find the others. It found the rocket and it went back to Earth. It killed 3,000,000 people and it then lay eggs in Grand Central Station before dying.

Cohen Williams (11)
Brownmead Academy, Shard End

Teddy

Ella had just come back from school when she noticed something different about the house. A teddy. "Why has my mum bought me a teddy? She knows I'm too old. But it wouldn't hurt if I played with it for a bit..." So Ella ripped open the teddy and read the instructions. It said, 'press the button and wish'. So she did. She wished for a dog. There, standing in front of her, was a dog. Just then she had an idea, she could wish for more teddies for her friends. So she did.

Zoyah Nadeem (10)

Brownmead Academy, Shard End

The Weird Forest

After seeing something crash, Captain America checked it out. He saw Thanos with his gauntlet. That meant war had started. At 7am, a portal opened up and Thanos was sucked up and was never seen again. Captain America was a hero and he was called a hero of the city. He was invited to a feast with the king. Captain America then got an upgrade on his shield and his armour, this meant that he was unstoppable.

Later that day, Thanos crashed back to Earth and he was never to be seen again...

Zack Henry Wilson (10)
Brownmead Academy, Shard End

The Alien That's Discovered After 2000 Years

In the year 2000 AD, the rare alien was discovered by some aliens just passing by. The rare alien was called Boo Boo. The scared aliens screamed because of the way Boo Boo looked. Then Boo Boo walked into a portal and his eyes adjusted to the bright world. There were weird-looking aliens who made him feel better. There were only ten rare aliens, they were 1,000ft tall and crushed people beneath them. He was a mean person, but do you think he could ever be nice to someone? What do you think?

Lacey Louise Welsh (11)
Brownmead Academy, Shard End

The Black Hole... To Toy Fantasy Land!

I saw a black hole on the ground. I tripped and fell right in! A quick adventure that I had ended in a flash. I looked around at myself and I seemed to look different. Toyland was where I was and I was one of them! Lego, dolls, action figures, this land had it all. I looked at myself once more to see my brick-looking body. I was a Lego person! I was now my favourite toy. I missed my mum and dad, I wanted to go home.

"Huh?" I was suddenly awake at home, it was just a dream!

Lacey-Lei Cheung (10)

Brownmead Academy, Shard End

The Man That Never Came Off The Moon

In 2097, there was a man called Marcus Armstrong who was always inspired by his grandad, Neil Armstrong. One tragic day, Marcus went to space with his partner Tomas. When they landed on the moon, they couldn't find Tomas anywhere. Then he saw a mysterious plate, it hit him like a train. It was a UFO! Marcus was then captured and he was put in a prison by the aliens. Tomas had been used as a spy. Soon, the whole universe would crumble down like crumbs falling off toast...

Tomas Alison Anderton (10)

Brownmead Academy, Shard End

Sam's Journal

It all started when Sam left home for the first time. It was the best experience she'd had in her life, going to Scotland, discovering new things, scrambling up Ben Nevis, jumping in a loch. Two people helped Sam during her trip: her favourite teacher and her friend Gabby. One thing they did was rock climbing and abseiling, which was scary. Also, they did zip lining which was as scary as you'd think at first because your heart's sinking through your body! Sam summed up the trip by saying, "It was scary for sure, fun and emotional!"

Mary-Kate Iheanacho (10)
Dulwich Wood Primary School, Dulwich

The Unknown King Of Planet Zy

One extremely hot day, an amazing phoenix was born. Luckily its parents were king and queen of Planet Zy. The phoenix was called Spare. Sadly, Spare's mum and dad died in a war with humans. Spare grew up and he knew there had to be another king, which was him, but not an ordinary king. His flashing, warm feathers shone brightly like the sun. Everybody bowed and as quick as a flash, the humans invaded. Sparks exploded into flames. The humans were defeated. Spare sacrificed himself for Planet Zy and then he was called the Unknown King.

Denisa Balint (9)
Dulwich Wood Primary School, Dulwich

The Magical Myths And Legends

Once upon a time, there was a unicorn called Safia and she had magical powers. Her friend Kia wanted to have a dance battle and Safia said yes because she wanted to cheat and get the trophy. All of a sudden, Kia realised that Safia was going to cheat with her magical powers. A goddess then came along and said, "There, there now, don't cheat because there are going to be consequences when you cheat."

Safia said, "I don't care. I'm going to cheat." So she did and she had to pay £1,000,000!

Markiah Scott-Bennin Alison (9)
Dulwich Wood Primary School, Dulwich

The Haunted Mansion Of Deric Death

Dear Diary,

Today me and Kate went to this haunted mansion. The legend said there was a ghost which belonged to Deric Death, a magician who could shape-shift. Unfortunately, he died by committing a dangerous, impossible stunt. Sliding under two chainsaws.

The door was open, so we went through. "Are you sure we should go?" Kate asked. I kept quiet and walked through as Kate quivered into the mansion. It was almost flooded with blood. As soon as we walked through the centre, a creature appeared: Deric Death.

Banjugu Kamara (9)

Dulwich Wood Primary School, Dulwich

The Black Hole

Once in space, there was a black hole and there was an astronaut who was also a scientist. He used some energy against the black hole but it wasn't strong enough.

One day, it was about to explode but then a man named Matthew John came and said, "Let me help you fix space."

The scientist got his astronaut suit on and they went into space. When Matthew got into space, he jumped into the black hole and he saw lots of things inside. He jumped out of it and it exploded but it didn't do anything.

David Duarte (10)

Dulwich Wood Primary School, Dulwich

Space In The City

A thousand miles away, there was a normal city until there was a big thunderstorm and lightning struck all the civilians. The city turned upside down, the sky on the bottom, the city on the top. Everyone felt sick at first but they got used to it. Three teens somehow stayed on the sky, they all got superpowers from the lightning. One was Eliza who had flight, Anika had indestructibility and Zach had ice powers. They fought off aliens but some of them were kind. They enjoyed it.

Eliza Rose Eachus (9)
Dulwich Wood Primary School, Dulwich

Slappy's Revenge!

One day, there were two children called Stella and Sunny. They were moving house next door to someone called Esme. They saw a ventriloquist's dummy called Slappy, but Stella and Sunny went for a playdate and found a locked book. They opened it and Slappy came out and said, "Who're your new friends?"

Stella whispered in Esme's ear, "Run!" so they ran. Esme said something that stopped Slappy. Slappy then said, "I'll get revenge and you'll regret it!"

Violet Matthews (9)

Dulwich Wood Primary School, Dulwich

Banishing Terror

Once there lived unicorns and dragons. They were always separated. I walked into a time machine, then suddenly, I heard a tiny unicorn squeak cutely. Apparently, the dragons started marching into the unicorns' land. All the unicorns were very scared, but I wouldn't let that happen. I amazingly turned into a magical fairy. What I did was use one of my magical spells to banish the dragons from the land. Sadly, the unicorns banished me because they'd asked the dragons to attack them. I was banished into a faraway land. I missed the unicorns because they were a family...

Ifetayo Bakare (8)
EP Collier Primary School, Reading

Princess Moonstone And The Curse

Alaska's kingdom has a princess named Moonstone who was cursed by a hermit to turn into a fireball dragon after sunset. The curse was a secret. The hermit wanted to marry her, but she refused his proposal. This made the hermit livid. From that day, Moonstone started to live in the forest. She felt scared but soon settled. At daytime, Moonstone got attacked by a dragon. The prince killed the hermit who was disguised as the dragon. The spell got broken and they both went to their kingdoms. Finally, she met her parents again after a long time.

Priyal Viral Khamar (8)
EP Collier Primary School, Reading

The Museum Mystery

The magic book of secrets had gone missing and Detective Simon was coming to solve it. As she entered the museum, she found a slimy, green trail and decided to follow it. Suddenly, the trail ended and she found herself in front of a gloomy tunnel filled with poisonous gas. After searching for a while, she was about to turn back when she heard a noise from above. When she looked up, a slimy substance fell on her face with a thud of the book. Suddenly, she heard a familiar voice, "Wake up, Simrah, or I'll pour more water!"

Simrah Merchant (7)
EP Collier Primary School, Reading

A Haunted House With Scared Rose

Once there was a girl called Scared Rose. One night, her parents left her all alone so she could watch TV for a little while, but then Scared Rose heard a spooky sound, it came to her ears. She got scared, then she heard a ghostly sound. She told herself that this place looked haunted and her parents shouldn't have left her behind. It was midnight, it was getting dark. Scared Rose got really scared, she heard a scream. She was terrified. Then the TV turned off. She got a spooky surprise...

Maham Faisal (7)
EP Collier Primary School, Reading

Mountainous Adventure

It all started when I went to Mount Budapest with my class as an adventure. We climbed to the top of the snow-capped mountain. We set up our campsite, warmed our hands and fell asleep. I was so interested in the flag in the east, I found myself climbing to it. I reached it and found myself surrounded by ghosts who wanted to kill me. I dodged and ran as fast as I could. I went to our campsite, telling my friends. All I knew was that nothing was as it seemed. I also got a big scolding.

Aarav Khasiwala (8)
EP Collier Primary School, Reading

Murder Mystery

One bright Monday, blood-curdling screams came from the haunted circus. The top detective of the police force came up and examined the scene. "Somebody killed this young lady!" proclaimed the detective.

They interviewed every single person at the fair and in her family. Nobody owned up. Everybody looked at the detective. Something was up with Alex because he wasn't looking at him. The detective figured Alex knew something. He told the detective that he was part of the gang that killed her. Little did he know, the detective was the one who killed Alisha Smith. No one suspected him, obviously...

Manha Ahmed (10)
Fairway Primary School, Mill Hill

Missing Adults

As I walked to the shop, there was something strange. The till lady was gone. I started freaking out. Suddenly, there was someone on the road, I was scared to talk to him. Then he was walking towards me. I shouted, "Go away!"
He said, "I'm not going to hurt you." He came and said the adults were gone. He told me to be his agent. "Come on, let's find the adults."
Two hours later, there they were. "Come back home!" I shouted. Then, I realised that it was all a bad dream...

Muqadur Juburkhil (9)
Fairway Primary School, Mill Hill

The Best Superhero

One day, a huge explosion occurred in the city. Superheroes arrived and for some odd reason, they started to fight. Out of nowhere came a robot villain. However, there was also a good robot. A superhero named Iron Man was very good and he had powers of which he could shoot fire blasts from his hands and his chest. He also had thick, steel armour protecting him from fatal attacks. Iron Man's quick thinking led him to rapidly kill the evil robot, saving everyone. Luckily, nobody was hurt during the evil robot's rampage.

Ylli Lushaku (8)
Fairway Primary School, Mill Hill

Slither

There was a boy named Dan, Dan was a twelve-year-old boy. Dan went to explore an abandoned hospital. He entered and the door opened with an unexpected creak. Dan had no idea what to think, he was haunted with fear. Then, his eyes saw something, it had broken arms and broken limbs. The creature stared at Dan, then started to chase him. Dan ran out of the hospital when suddenly, he tripped over. The creature then jumped onto Dan and ripped the flesh off him. His blood squirted like there was a bomb inside him.

Orson Lushaku (10)
Fairway Primary School, Mill Hill

You Won't Believe It

Once upon a time, there was a kid called Bob. He loved exploring and one day, a letter came in the mail and it said, 'would you like to help find buried treasure? It might take a few days but if that's okay, sign here'. Bob was excited and he went to his mum and asked if he could go on a mini trip with someone. She said yes.

The trip started the next day. Early in the morning, around six, Bob woke up and he went. He was there and they searched everywhere. Then Bob found the treasure...

Daniel Asadi (10)
Fairway Primary School, Mill Hill

Banana World

In this world, it rained bananas and there were so many, you could swim in them! The whole universe was yellow and rotten. This was good and bad, good because we wouldn't run out of food but bad because we would be drowning in bananas. This had to be stopped. All the people in the world got tons of wood, building up to the sky, and started to build a roof over the world to stop bananas falling. It took seven million years, but it was worth it. Bananas stopped falling from the sky around the world.

Kian Afshari Parsa (8)
Fairway Primary School, Mill Hill

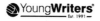

The Magic Dragon

There was once a dragon called Fred and he lived by himself because his parents died. This dragon loved space and he wanted to go to space. Fred liked science and wondered what the yellow thing was called. "When will I find out? I hope one day..." One day, the dragon walked down the street in Dragon World and he saw a dragon space shop which had a helmet. Luckily there was a £5 one in front of him. He bought everything in the shop and he sat on a toy spaceship and flew away!

Susanna Munns (9)
Fairway Primary School, Mill Hill

The Witch Who Tasted Revenge

Once upon a Halloween, there was a gruesome old lady at her door, giving out opened candy to everyone. One day, a girl called Agatha was told by the OSS to check out the house. When Agatha arrived there, she accidentally dropped the woman's vase, but with her super-fast reflexes, she caught it with her foot. She saw the elderly lady and she was making a potion. Agatha assumed she was a witch, so Agatha rushed back to headquarters and told everyone. The agents put the old lady in jail.

Ayub Mohamud Mohamed (10)

Fairway Primary School, Mill Hill

My Journey To Space

One late Saturday morning, me and two of my friends were ready for a journey to space. We went to the launch station and we saw the rocket, it was beautiful and lovely. Our rocket was named Apollo 11. After we entered the rocket, me and my friends took our seats. We started take off. We had ten seconds. After we took off, we were so happy because it was our first time in a rocket. After an hour in space, we saw a black hole. We really wanted to go back down to Earth, but we had to stay...

Mikaeel Inayatullah (9)
Fairway Primary School, Mill Hill

The Girl Who Turns Into A Superhero

There was a girl who was called Lilly. Her dream was to be a superhero. One day, she went to the kitchen and had a snack before she went to bed. She went to bed then when she looked in the mirror she screamed because she was a superhero! "Oh my gosh! Yay! I'm finally a superhero!" She ran downstairs and told her mum. Her mum said it was silly. "Mum! I have magic! It's unbelievable!" They were all happy. Lilly could do anything and everything! It was so cool.

Daisy Healey Thomson (9)
Fairway Primary School, Mill Hill

Five Nights At Freddy's

One stormy night, a little boy called Albert got trapped in a pizzeria. Albert always met friends who weren't real. He found out that he'd been trapped for ten years! As Albert was an expert math solver, he found out he was nineteen. Albert wanted to work here even though he didn't know if he could. The next day, Albert woke up in a dark room as a child and had to survive five nights starting from 12am to 6am. He skipped one night and he got eaten by an animatronic called Fredbear.

Reja Dilshad (9)

Fairway Primary School, Mill Hill

Super Duper Man Saves The City

The day started with me going shopping. I bought some toys, food and other stuff. Then, the ground started to shake, but then the shaking stopped. I looked up and I saw the top of the building was about to fall on me. After a few seconds, someone saved me! I didn't know him but then I saw his face. It was Super Duper Man! I was surprised. He got me back home and we had Christmas dinner together. We didn't want to leave him alone so we invited him to our party and we had a nice day.

Ianis Singurelu (8)

Fairway Primary School, Mill Hill

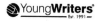

The Erupting Volcano

While I was exploring, I found an active volcano. It seemed okay at first. Some time later, the volcano started shaking and moving. Soon I realised that it was going to erupt at any minute, so I ran as fast as I could.

Eventually, I found out that the volcano wasn't going to erupt, it was just heating up. I went back to keep exploring and there I found a hot spring. I went in and suddenly felt a small fish!

Unfortunately, I found out that it was a piranha!

Armin Sarkoob (9)

Fairway Primary School, Mill Hill

Super Silly Space

Today is a big day for an astronaut, he has to go on the moon for the first time! He got on the moon and said, "Wow!" There was something super weird that looked like alien slime, it shot out of the floor. He found a rock and covered the hole, then something crazy happened. The moon was on fire! He quickly ran to his bag that was full of water. He put water all over the moon and he then went back to Earth. He had saved the moon!

Stefania Danila (8)
Fairway Primary School, Mill Hill

The Baby Unicorn's First Mission

Once there was a unicorn named Lilly. She grew up in a cottage nearby. She had the best day in her life. When it was getting close to her birthday, she was getting excited. She was jumping up and down which showed how excited she was for her birthday. She was excited so she went out to play and she found a pony stuck in a tree! It wasn't a tall tree so she could rescue the pony. Lilly was very excited because she had helped.

Roza Daif (9)
Fairway Primary School, Mill Hill

Sally's Adventure To Candy Land

I stepped into the magic door even though I didn't know what I was going to find. I looked everywhere but all I found was candy, just candy. I named the place Candy Land. As I got used to Candy Land, I made friends with gingerbread men, we played and we had tea parties.

When evening drew in, I went to have dinner with the gingerbread men. It was amazing! There was one thing I knew for sure and that was candy is amazing!

Maryam Gitey (8)
Fairway Primary School, Mill Hill

The One Time On The World

The boy's mum was nagging him to get off the TV. She wanted to go shopping. The boy wouldn't move from the TV until aliens invaded. The boy still didn't care, even though there was drama outside his house. Suddenly, Superman came out of nowhere and helped the people while the boy was still playing games. It was as if he was in a virtual reality. He did not care. He only thought about his game...

Gabriel Selimi (8)
Fairway Primary School, Mill Hill

Mysterious Horror!

Once I went to a mysterious forest with my family. I had a chance to step into the forest first and, as soon as I stepped in, everyone started to scream. I figured that there was a problem so I took a step back and then everyone stopped. I took a step again and I figured out that there was a mysterious figure behind me! I screamed and ran.

Maraam Bashraheel (8)
Fairway Primary School, Mill Hill

Going Camping

Dear Diary,

I can't wait until tomorrow because the whole class is going kayaking and we get to learn how to create a fire! Oh well, I'd better get to sleep. However, I'm absolutely starving. I hear something outside the tent, it sounds like it's eating something... I'm scared!

Dear Diary,

I decided to wake up one of my teachers. As the teacher unzipped the tent, she screamed. I dashed. With an empty stomach I was really exhausted. I ran aimlessly trying to find the cave. I stopped, realising that I hadn't brought the picnic basket... Should I go back?

Matheus Caoile (11)

Hareleeshill Primary School, Larkhall

Forest Nightmare

I walked through a freaky forest, not knowing what could be there. I heard footsteps. "Hello?" About twenty-five minutes later, I got dragged into a random house. "Argh! Where am I?" The house started shaking frantically as a big bang went off. "If I were you, I'd make a run for it!" a ghost said. I ran as quickly as I could until I tripped and fell. I was at that stage where I wanted to just faint, but before that happened, I heard nothing but the wind. I'd made it out of the forest nightmare...

John Mooney (12)

Hareleeshill Primary School, Larkhall

America At War With Germany

One day, there was a man named Pablo. He went to war and joined the American army. They went to war with Germany. He was very nervous and also scared because he was in a life-threatening moment. It was November when the war started. It was two days before Christmas and Pablo was worried that he would never return to his family. It was Christmas Day and both the Germans and the Americans came together and played football and had Christmas dinner. Then, both sides became friends. Then Japan came and America and Germany fought again.

Tyler McCallum (11)
Hareleeshill Primary School, Larkhall

Stuck In The Future

One day, two girls called Molly and Lilly were on their way to school. Then all of a sudden, they heard a noise in the woods so they decided to go see what the noise was. They saw a huge building. They went inside. Lilly saw the teleportation machine and decided to go inside. The door slammed behind her and she was stuck. The machine teleported her into the future. Molly realised that Lilly was stuck in the future and she started pushing buttons but they weren't working. Then she pulled a lever and Lilly finally came back!

Abi Douglas (11)

Hareleeshill Primary School, Larkhall

It's Messi!

I was so engrossed playing a game of FIFA on my Xbox that I didn't notice a bright beaming light forming around my television. A hand reached out, I couldn't believe my eyes... It was Messi! I took his hand and he pulled me into the game.

Everyone was chanting my name, "Jack! Jack! Jack! Jack!" The feeling was surreal. I thought it couldn't be happening! Before I knew it, Messi passed the ball and I managed to score a goal just before the final whistle. I had just scored the winning goal! The crowd went wild!

Jack Dingwall (11)
Hareleeshill Primary School, Larkhall

The Old Orphanage

The screams I heard were spine-chilling, making the hairs on my body stand up. What could it be? I was anxious to get out of my bed and look. It was dark, the dim lights from the orphanage made it hard to see the figure standing, looking up at me. Then from nowhere, the Greenlady I'd heard so many stories about was right beside me. I was petrified, I'd never imagined this ghost was real. My heart sank, my body was drenched with sweat. She suddenly disappeared. Was it just a dream or not...?

Lennox McLear (11)
Hareleeshill Primary School, Larkhall

The Unicorn Who Turned Into A Teddy

Once upon a time, a girl named Sophie went on a trip with her friends in the woods. They packed all their stuff into the cabin. After they packed all their stuff away, they went on a walk. Sophia started to see some suspicious things, but didn't tell her friends. At first, she saw a tail of some sort of horse, then a horn. She wasn't sure what it was. Then, her friends saw what she saw, it was a unicorn! They ran towards it and then hugged it. After they hugged it, it turned into a teddy.

Tilly Lindsay (11)
Hareleeshill Primary School, Larkhall

Voices

I was walking home from dance class one night, but I lost track of where I was going. I felt a sudden gust of wind through my hair. As I slowly turned around, not knowing what would be waiting for me, I screamed. The darkness was suddenly swallowing me! I bumped around until the rattling stopped. I opened my eyes to realise that I was alone once more. I could hear a voice calling me, coming from a creepy old mansion. It was pulling me. I came closer. I couldn't believe my eyes...

Brooke Kane (11)

Hareleeshill Primary School, Larkhall

Stolen!

Everything was going smoothly until Elana's friend Zoey said her bag had been stolen.

Elana told everyone to sit down and give an alibi.

Dan said, "I was with my girlfriend at the time, making up for not getting her a gift."

Then Elana turned to Anne who said, "I was getting some snacks at the time."

Finally, Alex said, "I didn't take it! I was being the DJ!"

Elana searched everyone's bags and saw Zoey's things in Dan's bag! "What is this doing here?" asked Elana.

Dan panicked and said, "I was going to give it back!"

Arabella Violet Mai Hughes (10)
Haughton St Giles CE Primary Academy, Haughton

The Battle Of Mars

I was in class learning about the gods, especially powerful ones like Mars and Neptune. Then something odd happened. I left school and thunder struck out of nowhere. It was Neptune! "Thy be god to Heaven!" he shouted and I found myself in what seemed to be Heaven. "Here, the lightning blade!" Next, I found myself on a quest to find Mars. It took a while with erupting volcanos and lava swamps. Finally, I got there. A fiery arena with flames and lava... There was Mars waiting for me. I prepared my sword and the battle began...

Jack George Marsh (9)
Haughton St Giles CE Primary Academy, Haughton

The Mermaid And The Girl

Once upon a time, there was a girl called Esme and she went to a beach and found a necklace. Esme thought that someone had lost their necklace, but when she looked at the sea, she saw a tail which was turquoise, her second favourite colour. Esme then saw a head and immediately knew it was a mermaid. The mermaid swam up to her and said, "My name is Splash."

Esme said, "My name is Esme."

Splash touched Esme and turned her into a mermaid with a pink tail, her favourite colour! That was it, she was a mermaid forever.

Leah Costley (8)
Haughton St Giles CE Primary Academy, Haughton

Adventure On A Horse To Find Some Treasure

One day, riding a horse called Mint, Emma went on an adventure to find some treasure. Emma was happily cantering along in the sunshine, Mint was being a good boy. Emma and Mint went into the forest to explore, they liked riding in the forest because they liked jumping logs. Emma and Mint were cantering in the middle of the forest, there was a bump on the floor. Emma dug it up and it was the treasure! The treasure was multicoloured jewels! They took it home and put it on the farm. It looked beautiful, Emma was very happy.

Emelia Allen (7)

Haughton St Giles CE Primary Academy, Haughton

Food Thief!

Once there was a hamster, he had a rival called Angus. One day, he discovered his hoard had vanished! He went on an investigation to find out what happened to his food. He left home and raced to Angus' palace. Surprisingly, Angus had no food! Stripe then set off to some other hamster homes. He then took Sky into questioning as she had a huge hoard. He asked her why she was late back home, she said she'd been to see him but he wasn't there. Stripe thought this was suspicious but she didn't go anywhere...

Beatrice Rose Palmer (9)
Haughton St Giles CE Primary Academy, Haughton

The Cave

Once there was a boy called Henry, he decided to go into the cave that was at the bottom of his enormous garden. It was not an ordinary cave, there was a light at the bottom and there lived a grumpy goat. The goat stood at the bottom of the cave, staring at Henry like a lion waiting for its prey. It took one look at him and the goat's coarse hair stood up on end. Its eyes glared back at Henry. Fright went through Henry's body, what could he do? Run for it or hide?

Henry Timmis (10)
Haughton St Giles CE Primary Academy, Haughton

Super Solo Space Mission

When I thought it was a good time to build a space rocket, I built it in my bedroom to shoot out of the window. Before I got started, I packed a bag. After I packed my bag, I got started on the spaceship. I went to the National Space Centre to ask if I could have an astronaut suit. The man there said yes. I then blasted off. I was zooming to space. I was holding on and I thought I saw a new planet. It was! I headed over to it.

Harry Marsh (7)

Haughton St Giles CE Primary Academy, Haughton

The Disappearance

One day, eight friends were at their high school and were assigned a spy to go to school with. That evening, one spy said, "School children are getting taken by someone and are disappearing."

Those eight friends went on Friday after school to find out who was taking the children. When they arrived at the school, there were clues everywhere. The spy also gave them gadgets and weapons. They split up into groups of two and went to investigate more clues, but when they met up, there were only five left. Where had the other three gone...?

Matthew Pope-Brannon (9)

Kessingland CE Primary Academy, Kessingland

The Day Pixie Turned Elf

Pixie was just an ordinary girl who found a mysterious door. This wasn't just any door, it was tiny. She saw a very scrunched up note on the table saying: 'Do not open the door or you'll disappear'. Pixie being Pixie didn't believe the note was true so she opened it. She felt a little tingle and tried to call her mum for help but she was too late. She appeared at a snowy field with a small gingerbread house. Upon closer inspection, she realised she was at the North Pole! She saw her reflection... She'd become an elf!

Daisy Jackson (9)
Kessingland CE Primary Academy, Kessingland

Billy The Legendary Mythical Creature

There once lived an ancient, ultimate mythical creature called Billy the Legendary. He was half-dragon, half-panda. He had sharp toenails and sharp fingernails. He could even shoot red lasers out of his eyeballs! His super speedy tail power helped him to sprint. There was so much more to his skills and appearance.

Billy fell through a portal, he didn't know where he would end up. Suddenly, he landed. He was in a fairytale universe. Then, someone looked at him. It was the ancient Spikey Mikey! Billy said, "It's over!"

Billy Willis (10)

Kessingland CE Primary Academy, Kessingland

Sock Monkey's Speedy Adventure

The train chugged faster and faster. Sock Monkey liked going super speedy in his tornado. Today he was extra speedy. Suddenly, there was a clang and a bang and a big flash of light. Shocked, Sock Monkey slammed on the brakes. They screeched loudly and came to a stop. He had stopped on a tropical beach and, to his surprise, there in the sand was an abandoned aeroplane. *Great*, Sock Monkey thought, and decided to see if it flew. He started it up and he was up, up and away, speeding happily once again through a beautiful blue sky.

Lewis Wilson Burgess (10)
Kessingland CE Primary Academy, Kessingland

The Haunted Girl

Once there was a teenage girl called Naiomi. Naiomi was a quiet girl who had no friends or anyone to talk to, however, she liked it this way because she had her own friend called Harry. He wasn't real though, he was imaginary but Naiomi liked to think he was real.

One night, a pale, transparent, freckled, red-headed boy showed up beside Naiomi's bed, staring directly down at her. Naiomi noticed something different about Harry, he had blood-red eyes that were never shut. Naiomi tried to run away, but she slipped on her shoelace...

Lacey Brookman (9)

Kessingland CE Primary Academy, Kessingland

The Island Trip

One day, I found myself on an island in the sand. I was scared but I went into the forest and saw animals like monkeys and sloths. I heard a noise, it was a man and he wasn't well. I grabbed plants to help him because a jellyfish stung him. Afterwards he was grateful because he could stand, walk and do things. He said, "Why don't we try and get off this island by making a raft?"
"Yes!" I replied. "That's a good idea."
When we'd made the raft, it floated away from the island.

Laila Young (10)
Kessingland CE Primary Academy, Kessingland

Co-Op Criminal

It was a snowy Sunday morning, Mikey was having a biscuit when his dog barked in alarm. Someone had robbed the Co-Op! Mikey slid outside, down the street to get to Co-Op quickly. When he got there, he started looking for clues, then he noticed a pile of biscuit crumbs on the floor. He followed the trail to the back room where he saw the door close. He went outside to discover the robber had stolen biscuits and the robber had started eating them. Mickey said, "You've been caught crumby-handed!" then sent the robber to prison.

Maddox Larter (10)
Kessingland CE Primary Academy, Kessingland

Demon Dentist Two

In the shadows, who everyone had thought was crushed to death, the tooth witch and her cat stepped out, still rattling like a skeleton. She was one. She looked around frantically and she ran up the hill and came into view. She saw the school where me and my friend Matthew go as the sun set behind it. Waiting in the distance, she stood, waiting for break-time so she could find her prey. As Matthew went to play, I was on my own. I turned around and spotted her... I screamed.

Hollie Mary Grace Chambers (9)
Kessingland CE Primary Academy, Kessingland

The World Of The Superheroes!

"Everyone! Gather around! The queen has sent a message. There is a party for the princess, every man is invited!"

All of a sudden, Austin came over! He was the most handsome man in the village. His biggest secret was that he was a superhero. So was Catherine, the princess of LA. Austin thought he was going to be the one to marry Catherine. He began to prepare but he couldn't dance, so he practised for a whole week. Then the final day came. Catherine and Austin fell in love and both superheroes lived happily ever after.

Malika Qurban (8)
North Walsall Primary Academy, Walsall

Fire Mission

Once there was a superhero called Watergirl, she had the power of water. One day, Watergirl was walking down the road until she saw her friend Icegirl. Icegirl was a really nice and caring friend to Watergirl. Then, when Watergirl and Icegirl got to school, they were ten minutes late, so they had to go to Mrs Price who was the headteacher. They got in trouble.

After school, Watergirl saw Firegirl setting roads on fire. Watergirl squirted the road that was on fire with water and Icegirl froze Firegirl and she was arrested.

Evie Weseley (9)

North Walsall Primary Academy, Walsall

Mystery Someone

On a cold, miserable night, I heard a spooky sound that caught my attention. Everything felt suspicious like someone was watching me. As I walked towards the window, I could hear the loud water droplets and the gushing wind. Then there was a creaky sound in the floorboards. It made me feel like I wasn't alone, someone was in the house! I came out the room and went downstairs to see if anyone was there, but no one was. I heard ferocious banging at the door and, as I went towards the door, I felt a hand on my shoulder.

Eliza Akhtar (9)
North Walsall Primary Academy, Walsall

A Princess Surprise

The princess went to sleep, dreaming of magical things like rainbows, unicorns and butterflies. She woke up to her father saying, "I have a surprise for you!" He took her downstairs, she saw a unicorn! She pinched herself but she didn't wake up. She went to stroke the unicorn and she and the unicorn became best friends. Sometimes, she would ride the unicorn but then, she woke up. It was all just a dream. She was so sad and she wished that she could have the dream once more...

Naomi Smith (9)
North Walsall Primary Academy, Walsall

The Mystery Of The Man

At a party on Saturday, a weird man came. He went outside and he disappeared. People started to look for him outside but they couldn't find him. A girl stopped the party and said, "I saw a man two minutes ago. He's gone now, we need to find him and know what happened." They investigated all night and morning but they couldn't find him. Would they ever find him?

Habibah Bibi (8)

North Walsall Primary Academy, Walsall

The Haunted House

One extremely stormy night, there was an adventurous little red ghost that found a haunted house. It had vines all over the windows and the door was rusted shut. Obviously, he was a ghost so he just went right through it. He didn't shiver in fear, he was feeling too exhilarated about what he could find. Within seconds, he became aware of something sticking out of a hidden hole. A dirty wooden lever which opened a secret door! Thinking about where the secret door led to, he hovered down a spiral staircase and, after that, he was never seen again!

Jack Thomas Boyce (10)
Oakwood Primary School, Glasgow

Below The Sea

Below the sea, there lived a magical mermaid called Sienna. Sienna was able to change her tail colour to camouflage herself from the evil octopus that wanted to kill her. Sienna was calmly swimming around the sea when she spied the octopus coming towards her. She sneakily hid behind a massive rock and changed her tail from a light green to a dark grey. Sienna was hoping the octopus would swim in the other direction. Sienna thought she was alone, but then she felt something touch her. It was the octopus! She screamed at the top of her lungs...

Ellie Longridge (10)
Oakwood Primary School, Glasgow

Bear's Adventure

One dark soaking night, Bob and I were looking out my bedroom window. We saw a tiny bear in the woods. She looked lost. We decided to go rescue her and bring her back to our cosy cottage. Straight away, we noticed she was shivering so we wrapped her in my fluffy, pink housecoat. Hot chocolate seemed like a good idea until the microwave blew up. Feeling annoyed, we stomped to bed. After a good night's sleep, we felt hungry so we ordered Nutella pancakes from Poppy's Pancakes. They tasted delicious. The bear then became part of our family.

Karra Norman (10)

Oakwood Primary School, Glasgow

Into The Future

I felt terrified as I was sucked into a magical board game called Save the Future. As I closed my eyes, I entered this unknown place. The sky was yellow with brown clouds. From a distance, I saw a tree, it had a carving which said '7020' so I screamed. *Bang!* A fierce-looking man holding a gun appeared, aiming it at me! "I think I have to save the future..."

More spotted me. What could I do? As I became more anxious, I felt a sudden movement. I looked and I had blue wings. I flew and attacked...

Kaisey-Lee Rae (9)

Oakwood Primary School, Glasgow

Be Aware

I suddenly stepped towards something dark and spooky. It was a haunted house! It was really scary. I sprinted as fast as a cheetah to the old, rusty door. As I approached the door, something screamed in my face. I jumped with fear, shivers down my back. I felt something touch me, but nothing was there. What was happening to me? I asked myself if it was a ghost. I was flabbergasted, wanting to scream but I was speechless. Someone pulled me up, but I couldn't see them because they were invisible. I just wanted to go home!

Lucy Rooney (10)
Oakwood Primary School, Glasgow

The Huge Triceratops

As soon as I stepped into the beeping time machine, I travelled three million years into the past. Everything looked the same until I saw monkey bars, they were tall and, if you fell, you would fall into a pool. Then, I turned and saw a chute three times the size of the monkey. I climbed up and saw something even bigger. A triceratops with roughly forty spikes! I'd never seen anything so scary but after a while, I noticed it was a friendly dinosaur. Everyone chanted, "Triceratops!" When it came past, everyone loved it!

Lewis McKenzie (9)
Oakwood Primary School, Glasgow

The Spooky Ghosts

It was a dark, stormy night. I was walking to my gran's house to stay overnight. I felt terrified because there was nobody about. I hurried into my gran's old scary-looking house. She was frightened by my footsteps and came towards me with a tennis racket in her hand. When she realised it was me, she felt relieved. My gran sent me upstairs to bed but I sneaked up the ladder to the loft instead. In the loft, I found boxes of my gran's childhood memories. As I opened one of the boxes, I heard a rattle...

Lucy Thomson (10)
Oakwood Primary School, Glasgow

The Familiar Noise

When I was seven, my mum and dad bought me a happy hamster for my birthday. I called him Chip because he looked like a chocolate chip cookie. Now I'm nine and it's my tenth birthday tomorrow, so I'm very excited!

I wake up to the worst sight of my life. Chip is dead! I'm devastated, but Mum tells me to wait in the car. On the way to the car, I hear a familiar noise. It sounds like Chip's wheel but he's dead... or so I thought. I look to discover it was a nightmare! Chip's alive!

Chantelle Catherine Blyth (10)

Oakwood Primary School, Glasgow

Alien Abduction

After a while, my eyes opened and I saw myself on a weird planet. I looked around to see what planet I was on. It was Mars! Unexpectedly, I felt like a ghost because there was no oxygen. I saw an alien, it had a moustache and a long tail. It was crazy because aliens didn't exist. Tons of UFOs were soaring through the sky. Suddenly, I was abducted from Mars and taken to Venus. I heard aliens talking but it sounded different from my language. Adrenalin was running through every part of my trembling body...

Junior Allan (10)
Oakwood Primary School, Glasgow

The Meteor Shower

As I touched the sphere, it teleported me to a black and white world where the only coloured objects were meteors which were as slow as a sloth. When they hit the ground, they didn't explode, instead, they created a splash of colour but only where they hit. After a while, watching the meteors fall, I decided to look for a way to leave this world. I was asking everyone but no one knew how. I was losing hope. Then I had an idea. If I were splashed by a meteor, I could go home! I tried... and it worked!

Owen White (10)

Oakwood Primary School, Glasgow

Fairies From Nowhere

I had nothing to do except play by myself or go outside to eat the tasty fruit from the berry tree. Unexpectedly, as I looked out, two fairies appeared and started munching my berries. I shouted at them, but they were staring at me blankly. After I opened the door, I slowly tiptoed up to them. They hid behind the tree, looking terrified. I scooped some fallen berries from the pale, sparkly pink grass using my magical horn. I placed them carefully on my back and waited for them to fly over to me...

Amy Collins (10)
Oakwood Primary School, Glasgow

No Way Home But One

I am in a lodge practising for the talent show when a floorboard creaks and I jump with fear. I run into a closet and turn around. I am in a different world! Where am I, I wonder. I run like a cheetah, my heart is pounding with sweat running down my back. I trip on something, it's a brick with smudged words on it. After a few minutes, they become clearer. It says, 'time machine'. Out of the blue, I'm back in the lodge. I run home, thinking *I'll never go there again!*

Kayleigh Duncan (10)
Oakwood Primary School, Glasgow

The Haunted House In Town

During the night, a little girl went trick or treating and went to a massive house in town. She went up the creaking, spooky staircase and rang the doorbell. Slowly, the door began to open, but no one was there. She went into the house and said, "Hello?" When she went in, the door slammed behind her. She just carried on. Then she felt something behind her and it was a clown chasing her. Then, a toy came and helped the clown. Then a ghost came and helped her escape from the house.

Casey Etherson (10)
Oakwood Primary School, Glasgow

A Whole New World

As I leapt out of my owner's ruby-red car, I noticed a weird-looking door. It was pale pink with glitter on it. I was curious to see what was behind the door, but the pathway was mucky. I had to get my paws dirty. When I pushed the door open, a bright light flashed right before my eyes, so I ran as quick as a flash through the strange door. As I looked around this world, I saw houses made of gingerbread, trees that were scented, lakes of syrup and glittery rain...

Oliwia Kurowska (10)
Oakwood Primary School, Glasgow

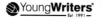
Draco's Howler

Resting far away near the mountains, Hogwarts School sat with children inside learning magic. In the school, the Great Hall spread across most of the building. Stumbling to her seat, Hermione felt embarrassed because Draco defeated her using Stupefy in Quidditch. Slithering like a snake, a Howler arrived in Draco's face! Lips appeared and abruptly screamed at Draco saying he had been the naughtiest person in the school.

"Draco Malfoy! Go to my office *now* to talk!"

In a split second, Professor Snape came in, took Draco by the wrist and walked off with him. Hermione, Ron and Harry ran!

Mia Priddis (10)
Rockbeare CE Primary School, Rockbeare

The Case Of The Disappearance And Discovery Of A Diamond Ring

At French Blossom boarding school for girls, Linda, April, Emily and Leah all played. Meanwhile, Miriam was upstairs brushing her hair. Madame le Pointe was fussing over makeup. All was well... Dramatically, a scream sounded and terror reached their eardrums! Leah bounded up the grand staircase to investigate. April fainted while Lucinda crumpled into a heap, sobbing salty tears! Emily draped herself in the curtains. Bravely, Leah trampled cautiously across the hall and into Miriam's room. Like a swooping eagle, the room had endured an attack! The window was open and a diamond ring was caught on the latch...

Evangeline Exell (9)

Rockbeare CE Primary School, Rockbeare

Why?

"Hey, come back here!" shouted Widow at the thief.

Widow was a spy with a murky past. She was going to find the truth that was hidden. Widow was just a finger's touch away from him when she heard the police. She was stuck in a dark gloomy alley in the middle of nowhere! "Hey, Dad! Come back!" she heard someone shout.

It was her sister. *How could you know that?* she asked herself. After a couple of minutes, they caught him!

"Why, Dad? Just why?" asked Widow.

"Well, I just..."

The truth slipped out. He was a criminal.

Ruby Curran (10)

Rockbeare CE Primary School, Rockbeare

Reaper Takes Over!

Amaya found herself being pulled out of bed. Her eyes were opened by a bony finger. It was Reaper, her skeleton half! The next thing she knew, he was opening a door. A frozen breeze hit her flesh half. Suddenly, a ghost flew overhead. She was in the death realm! All of a sudden, Reaper went wild and started running around the gravestones singing a chant. Hands and legs started to sprout from the ground! He was waking the dead! Then a glimmer of light hit the shrivelled grass. Amaya suddenly realised she was not home! She was trapped!

Temperance F (10)
Rockbeare CE Primary School, Rockbeare

The Escape

Once lived a boy called Jack Smith. Jack lived with his grandparents. It was a horrible life for a ten-year-old. They were cruel old people putting poor Jack to work. They treated him more like a slave than a grandson! So one day when he was meant to be mowing the grass, he snuck away. Running down the hill, Jack felt free for the first time since his parents had died. Running down into the woods, he hid behind a tree. Then from behind the tree, he saw a long bony hand! It was his favourite uncle, Uncle Roy...

Charlie Moore (10)
Rockbeare CE Primary School, Rockbeare

The Woods

As James entered the woods, it felt like he was being watched. The trees were alive and arguing like people with different personalities. Flaming below his feet lay the crisp, damp leaves; these stabbing, searing spears of sizzling fire spread across the dense ground. Mother Nature was at its best. However, he could hear the sounds of machine guns hiding behind the trees in the distance! He had to move.

Frightened, he began to run, dodging the sixty-foot-tall trees. His heart was racing...

Amy Bourne (11)

Rockbeare CE Primary School, Rockbeare

The First Alien

Before you were born in 1762 aliens came to Earth! There was one man who discovered it... One morning a man called Bob wanted to have an adventure. So he walked out of his home and conveniently he saw an alien ship! He was amazed. He'd known there were aliens out there since he was two years old. The search for the alien began! After three days, he found a trail of footprints to a cave. He tiptoed into the cave and he turned around and saw... An alien! Bob was ready to take a picture...

Connor Davey (10)
Rockbeare CE Primary School, Rockbeare

The Day Of Dalek Invasion!

When Mina stepped into the hotel doors, she could only find one thing that could speak. A robot. Her dog, Snowy, was growling. Mina knew that the robot must be horrible! "Who are you?" a rusty voice said.

"I'm Mina, who are you?" she said.

"We-are-the-Daleks!"

Everybody was silent.

"Exterminate!" it cried.

"Argh!" everybody screamed.

"You! Mina, come!" it said.

"No!" she cried.

The Dalek pushed her dog into a room and trapped it.

"Snowy, no!"

Mina got angry. She dodged all of the death beams and pushed the Dalek over...

Daisy Taylor (9)

Rossington St Michael's CE Primary School, Old Rossington

Rainbow Ninja And The Murderer

Boom! Flash! Thunder and lightning filled the sky. I heard a bullet firing before a horrendous scream filled the whole street. My curiosity got the better of me as I strolled towards the echoing scream. I suddenly stumbled across a deep, dark valley where a body lay flat, face-down on the concrete path. I nudged the woman and saw the bullet-hole where she had been shot. I was shocked! I spied a gun next to her. I became suspicious and realised something. A killer had been here! They were after me next! "Arghhh!" I ran in panic...

Constance Rose-Tottie (9)

Rossington St Michael's CE Primary School, Old Rossington

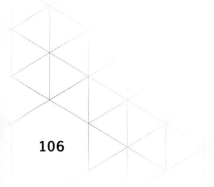

The Boy Who Dreamt Of Being An Astronaut

One day a boy dreamed of being an astronaut. He knew about Neil Armstrong, Buzz Aldrin and Michael Collins' mission. His dream came true! He woke up not knowing where he was. He looked around the spacecraft and then he noticed he was in the spacecraft with Piers Sellers, Helen Sharman and Michael Foale. They said, "Hi!" to the boy and then Piers Sellers, Helen Sharman and Michael Foale helped him. It was around 1972 when the boy went on the mission. They were going to the moon! Pieces of the moon flew around in space...

Jessica Littlewood (10)
Rossington St Michael's CE Primary School, Old Rossington

The Haunted House

One day there was a haunted house near a lake. By the way, I am Frank. Me and my mates always pass the house when we go to school. There used to be an old woman that lived in the house but she moved out a year ago. She had curly hair and was nice to others. She lived with a dog and her grandchildren. They moved with her. Her grandchildren were called Millie and Joe.

One day when they were gone, we found out there was some sort of creature in the house...

Victoria Karolina Mirga (9)

Rossington St Michael's CE Primary School, Old Rossington

The 'D' Robbers

Crash, bang, wallop! The fence collapsed, booming down to the ground. The dogs were on a mission, a dangerous mission! Gunner and Trigger were the town robbers. "Quick! Let's go to the bakery!" Trigger barked.

"That's a great idea! Let's go!" replied Gunner.

The dogs raced down the pavement, their paws thundering on the ground. They finally reached the bakery. They stole all the food and even a bottle of Coke! They thought their mission was over but just as they left through the door, a police dog arrived in a police car! They arrested them for their whole lives!

Evie Medlicott (11)

Rushbury CE Primary School, Rushbury

The Night Of Nothing...

"Hey, Liam. Do you want a game of football?"
"Okay, let's play!"
When they started playing, Liam saw a flash of light in the cinema window. The boys chose to go through the cinema door. They saw black figures slowly walking towards them... More appeared in the darkness! Suddenly, the cinema screen flickered and ghosts rushed out of the screen, running towards them! They were very scared so they tried to escape. Zombies and ghosts were coming from all directions! They had no choice but to run for their lives! *Boom!* There was nothing. They were never seen again.

Edward Noblet (8)
Rushbury CE Primary School, Rushbury

Minecraft World!

"Can I play on Minecraft, Mum?" I screamed.
"Go on, but don't play for too long, you'll get square eyes!"
"Okay!"
I ran to the computer and as quick as a flash, I was playing on Minecraft. Then it went fuzzy. I blinked and there in front of me was a black square portal that suddenly pulled me in! I was in Minecraft! I was actually kind of enjoying it. I realised that I could go from the normal world into the Minecraft world! I didn't want to do it with my brother's Zombieland games, they are extremely scary!

Freya Bromley (8)
Rushbury CE Primary School, Rushbury

The Tasty Adventure

My teacher was talking all about fractions *again!* I was so bored, I started to chew my pencil. It tasted sweet. My pencil case did as well. Everything did. I tried my table. It tasted like chocolate! I could not stop. I ate another table. My jumper tasted like jelly beans, paper tasted like shortbread. I took a bite of my finger. It was delicious!
"Katie! Katie, wake up!"
It was my teacher's voice. I woke up. I had been daydreaming! Well, that's what fractions make you do. Daydream. I wished Candy Land was real...

Katie Northwood (7)

Rushbury CE Primary School, Rushbury

The Magic Unigirl

Once upon a time there lived a girl called Ellie. She went for a walk and saw a pink door. She opened it. "Wow!" Ellie gasped. On the other side of the door was a gathering of mythical creatures! Ellie felt something heavy on her head. She touched her head and felt a horn! She realised she was a unigirl! Ellie made friends with the creatures. "Oh no!" Ellie said. "I have to go!"

She opened the door and walked back sadly. She got home.

"What have you been doing?"

"Oh, nothing," said Ellie.

That was a super, spectacular adventure!

Isabella Whale (8)

Rushbury CE Primary School, Rushbury

The Magic Stone...

One sunny day a girl was walking along the street and she stepped on something hard. It was small, shiny and looked unusual. She picked it up and put it in her pocket. As she walked home, she realised that every time she put her foot down, it didn't actually touch the floor. She could hover! She played about a bit and before she knew it, she could actually fly! When she got home, she put the object on the table but then her flying powers stopped. She could only fly when holding the shiny object. "I really love this!"

Darcey Jayne Blackwell (7)

Rushbury CE Primary School, Rushbury

Leaper Girl Saves The World

I'm Leaper Girl, top superhero. I have a sidekick called Turbo Turtle. Suddenly, my buzzer went off! Master Meanypants was taking over the city with bubblegum. I had to act fast! I rushed home and fetched a needle. When I got back, Turbo and I raced towards the bubblegum. I leapt onto the bubblegum and pricked it with my needle! It burst! We raced off, pricking and popping as we went. Then I saw Master Meanypants standing near me. I called the police immediately and poked Master Meanypants on the bottom. That was the end of him!

Eleanor Merrill (8)

Rushbury CE Primary School, Rushbury

Kind-Hearted

The evening was cold. There was a damp smell creeping up from the pavement. The elderly man tried to keep warm, huddled in a doorway with a rug pulled up to his chin. He watched as people walked home from work with coffee and snacks, hoping someone would give him something to eat. Eventually, a man tossed him a doughnut. His mouth began to water but then he spotted a child in rags. He took pity on the girl and gave her the doughnut. "Thanks, Mister!" she said. "Your costume is great, are you going trick or treating too?"

Josie Wilson (11)
Rushbury CE Primary School, Rushbury

The Ghost Chase

Once upon a time Harry and Hermione were walking down the corridor and accidentally walked into a ghost. The ghost was so angry, it started to chase them! The ghost chased them past their home through the green forest until they got to the frozen river. There was a massive tree and ghosts couldn't climb or fly. They climbed the tree rapidly and cast a spell on the ghost to send it back to where it came from! When they got back to the castle, they ran upstairs! They were exhausted so they got into bed.

Isabel Frost (9)
Rushbury CE Primary School, Rushbury

Ghost House

"I dare you to go in the haunted house!" said Sam.
"But I don't want to... Hm, okay, fine," said Linda
nervously.
All of the children then went into the house. Sid
found a shiny key in the dust and noticed a
keyhole shining. So Linda put the key in the hole.
Suddenly, all the ghosts of the town floated out!
They had been released after hundreds of years!
The people on Earth now had to learn to live with
ghosts that would haunt them all the time. Some
bad, some good, and some very naughty...

Hannah Price (7)
Rushbury CE Primary School, Rushbury

The Curse

I saw a flash. I accelerated until my legs went to jelly and I collapsed to the slimy, muddy and wet ground. I saw a figure in the puddle. It touched my shoulder. I looked behind me. It was a clown! Without a sound, I stood up and brushed myself down and realised I had been cursed to a clown! I had red curly and frizzy hair. I was weirdly on a cloud but then I tried to get up and I couldn't! Nervously, I looked back up and there was a banner saying 'You're dead'. I closed my eyes...

Ryleigh-Mae Young (10)
Rushbury CE Primary School, Rushbury

Snowy Adventure

My family and my dog were on a winter's walk in the mountains with hats and gloves on. It was very cold now. The snow was up to my waist! Suddenly, the snowy floor opened and we all fell down a large hole! We were screaming. It was terrifying. The screaming eventually turned into laughter. We realised it was fun! My dog jumped up onto my knee and then we came to the end of the tunnel. We went back to the start to do it again because it was the most exciting adventure we'd ever had!

Isla Grace Hercock (7)
Rushbury CE Primary School, Rushbury

X Rampage

2000 years ago there lived a man called Leo. He did not want to be a superhero. He wanted to move from the Hero House School. There was a boy called Isaac who liked being a superhero and enjoyed Hero House School. Leo had spent 2000 years training to be a villain instead and wanted to destroy all the people. So Isaac transformed into a flash of light and into a wave to stop Leo! Then Leo transformed into an X villain wave...

Isaac Stokes (7)

Rushbury CE Primary School, Rushbury

I Squeeze My Hands

I squeezed my hands tightly together. I opened my eyes and started to look around. Neon lights flashed, making my eyes hurt. A pawn shop was on my right. I slowly peeked my head around the graffitied wall. I was in New York City! I was pushed out of the alley and onto the street. I saw a big, tall building. It was really majestic. A red-rusty car bundled past. I started to run away. Soon I arrived at the edge of the road. It was scary. I squeezed my hands tightly shut. Imagine if you could teleport! *Pop...*

Dan Martin (9)
St John's Priory School, Banbury

New York City With Me And My Dad

I was hiding in New York City from my dad. We were playing hide-and-seek. He was far behind. I found a good hiding spot but my dad was getting closer!

I came out and looked at the green, tall Statue of Liberty. My dad stood next to me! Suddenly, he found me.

Then we went inside the Statue of Liberty. After that, we explored. We saw lots of graffiti. We had a great time. We went everywhere. We loved the big, tall Statue of Liberty with an amazing colourful inside! I had lots of fun. I love New York!

Evangelie Fisher (8)

St John's Priory School, Banbury

Klara's New York City Adventure

I squeezed my eyes and when I opened them, there were lots of different sounds around. *Bang!* Me and my mum were surrounded by people that were shouting and screaming. Lots of animals were making sounds too! I couldn't stand it anymore and my mum hated it too. Then a handsome man came and told us we were in New York.

"I want to go to The Statue of Liberty!" I said to my mum.

"Taxi!" shouted my mum.

A big yellow taxi zoomed up to us and we got in. It was great fun there!

Klara Jamrozinska (8)
St John's Priory School, Banbury

Grand Canyon

I squeezed my eyes closed as I saw brown water splashing up at me. I was at the Grand Canyon. I was sitting on a rock. A boat flew past. I jumped, hoping to get on! I swam and got pushed onto rocks. *How did I get here?* I guessed I could teleport! I was so close to the boat. Finally, I was safe! Waving my hands in the water was great. *Sizzle! Pop!* I was back in the classroom, my teacher was writing on the board. No one even noticed I had gone anywhere! Where would I go next?

Maya Rose McManus (8)

St John's Priory School, Banbury

Space Detectives: Mobile Phone

"The engine, I don't know why, but it's broken!" said Astro. Stranded in space, could anything else go wrong? Yes! Now they were under attack by the crime masters! The space detectives abandoned the ship, not realising that the ship was on pod lockdown.

"What about our mobile phone?" said Astro. "We can program it to install the back-up pod."

They were able to escape the crime masters by turning the pod into a time machine and travelling away to a new year, wondering what new adventures they would find. The space detectives finally won against the crime masters. Hooray!

Noah Couldridge (9)

St Joseph's Catholic Primary School, Hertford

Earth, Space And Beyond!

Once upon a time there lived a shepherd with some sheep. The shepherd was taking them out one day and one of the sheep escaped and ran off! When he stopped running, he found himself at NASA. He walked around until he found a rocket. He climbed inside and the rocket took off! The rocket automatically strapped him in.

After a couple of hours, they landed on the moon! The sheep said, "One giant leap for man, one massive leap for sheep-kind!" He put a flag on the moon. Then he got back in the rocket and landed on Earth.

Shay Lawlor (9)

St Joseph's Catholic Primary School, Hertford

The Mystery Of John's Death!

I heard the news and was right there. It was in the creepy house. My brother John was dead and I was on the case. I looked at CCTV and I saw my uncle Bobney leaving the house. I was determined to hunt him down and find out what happened. I finally found him in Cambridge. I asked him what he was doing. He said, "I killed your brother and I'll kill you!"

I held my hands together and blasted him with all my might. Bobney went to prison and I, Mystro, went into hiding again. Everything was normal.

Lilian Lunness (9)
St Joseph's Catholic Primary School, Hertford

Attack Of Alien Sheep

Alien sheep were attacking Earth! Jake was fighting the horde off but suddenly he got abducted and taken to Planet Zorgo, the planet of the alien sheep! Then Jake saw that the sheep were eating his friends. Suddenly, Jake jumped up and sliced the leader sheep! It only sliced his wool off and it regrew straight away! Then Jake ran away and found yellow balls with red stars on them. He threw them at the leader sheep! It shrunk him and then shrunk the rest of the sheep! Then the world was saved thanks to Jake.

Edison Murray (10)

St Joseph's Catholic Primary School, Hertford

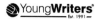

War Of All Wars

Across the galaxy far away there were two planets. There was a poor boy who had a dream. It was to go to another world. For a poor boy like him, would it ever happen? On the other world to his, there was a war going on. Megabot the evil robot then started a war on the boy's planet!
Four days later, Megabot set his army on the boy! The boy tried to get to the mega-ship to kill all of the robots but Megabot found him! He said, "Fight!" They fought and then Megabot killed him.

Harry Serjeant (9)

St Joseph's Catholic Primary School, Hertford

The Bald Bush

Once upon a time there was a snake that never left a bush. It wasn't just any bush, it was a bush with no leaves. All the explorers didn't dare go near the bush. It was titled 'The Bald Bush'.
One day an explorer called Alex looked at the bush and heard a burning noise. He looked closer. There was a fire! He went to the nearest river and filled a bucket with water. He tipped it on the bush. Alex took the snake home and now he has a pet snake! He is happy with his life.

Gabriella Hunte (10)

St Joseph's Catholic Primary School, Hertford

Christmas Magic

"Lights, lights and more lights!" shouted Kenny from upon the roof.

It was finally Christmas and little five-year-old Kenny, her older brother, her mom and her dad all decorated their house. Kenny's dad shouted, "No more lights! We will blow a fuse!"

All of a sudden, there was a loud bang! Then it went dark.

"Too late now," Kenny said giggling to herself.

Dad came down from the roof and said, "Don't worry, I'll sort it."

Suddenly, the lights came shooting back on! They all decided that they'd had enough lights and went inside for hot chocolate and marshmallows. Yum!

Ruby Jane Skett (10)
St Margaret's At Hasbury CE Primary School, Hasbury

Football Saves The World!

The three Villa players watched in amazement as the alien craft landed. Jack Grealish couldn't believe his eyes! Purple aliens!

"We want to play football!" said Alien 1.

"Okay," said Mings.

"If we win, we win your Earth!" said Alien 2.

So they played. The match was tense! John McGinn scored the first goal. Then Alien 3 scored from an epic free kick!

"Arghhh!" said Mings.

At eighty-eight minutes, it was still 1-1. The Earth appeared doomed! Suddenly, Jack Grealish came charging up the pitch and smashed the ball into the top corner! Villa Park cheered. The Earth was saved!

William Dennis Fairclough (10)
St Margaret's At Hasbury CE Primary School, Hasbury

The Unknown

Trees danced to the howling wind whilst the leaves pirouetted like ballerinas. While marching through the bloodstained, shivering grass, Amber searched for clues. Just twenty-four hours ago in that very spot, someone was killed! Huge footprints were imprinted in the foresty ground. Amber observed and took samples of the imprints. However, it was an unknown species! Burnt bushes surrounded the scene and vast maple trees were left lying on the uneven ground. Whatever the monster looked like, it was definitely big! Amber was absolutely bewildered. She had never seen such clues like this! All the signs pointed to something unimaginable...

Zahra Gul (11)

St Margaret's At Hasbury CE Primary School, Hasbury

Back To The Past!

Early one misty, stormy day, Andrew, a determined explorer, received messages about his latest mission sent from MI6. Of course he was an explorer, not a killer, but this was no ordinary mission, this involved great courage and large amounts of confidence. He was told to create a portal which could teleport him to various countries on Earth! A few minutes later, Andrew collected his list of ingredients: T-rex skull, diamonds and steel. At that moment, he realised something did not look correct...
Whoosh! Bang! He could see flying cars zooming. *Boom!* "What on Planet Earth just happened?" he gasped.

Mohammed Ibrahim Hussain (10)

St Margaret's At Hasbury CE Primary School, Hasbury

The Fawn And The Humans

Coolly, I crawled carefully through the miniature door expecting nothing. However, as my eyes examined the area I saw strange aliens talking. Then I realised they were humans and the door disappeared! A number of humans were glaring at me. Strangely the horrible humans had no hooves whatsoever! Forehead sweating, I dashed like my life depended on it through a never-ending hallway. Suddenly, I stumbled! Edging backwards, my twisted hoof was aching. Without hesitation, a young maiden held out her hand. Shaking, I took it. Relieved, I smiled broadly. I then realised humans are kind-hearted.

Alyssa Marie Bodin (10)

St Margaret's At Hasbury CE Primary School, Hasbury

The Night At The Graveyard

My heart was thundering. The spirits of the people surrounded me like I was in a box. All I could hear was my own breath. As I walked deeper into the endless graveyard, I heard a cackle. It almost sounded like... a witch! I went to investigate more. Surprisingly, a witch somehow teleported right in front of me!

"Who are you?" I shot out enthusiastically.

She just ignored me and walked crookedly away. *Is this a dream?* I pinched myself to see if it was a dream but it wasn't! *What should I do now? I want to escape...*

Malak Salih (9)

St Margaret's At Hasbury CE Primary School, Hasbury

Spooked

I walked closer into the dark cold forest, thinking about what was lurking around in the nettles. Something scurried across the floor. An owl hooted and as quick as a flash, I ran! Branches whacked my face. A dead end! A discarded barn was in front. I tucked myself inside. A roar came from the distance. Was it Death Blood? He had twenty-eight heads, thirty legs and eighteen arms! I heard a *stomp, stomp, stomp!* It was coming closer through the roaring wind! I shuddered, my arms wrapped around me. I wanted to go home but I was lost...

Anais Olivia Palmer (9)

St Margaret's At Hasbury CE Primary School, Hasbury

Chased At Night!

Moonlight ran like the wind. She knew she was being chased but she was losing pace. Her legs ached and her fur was standing on end! Hours had passed and Moonlight was starting to panic. She could hear the wolves howling behind. They wanted her but she didn't know why. She glanced back at the bright yellow eyes. They were gaining on her! Suddenly she shot into a clearing. Up ahead, Moonlight could see a dark, shiny lake. This could be her only chance to escape! She took a deep breath and plunged in! Darkness swallowed her up... Finally safe!

Molly Varney (9)

St Margaret's At Hasbury CE Primary School, Hasbury

Sady Hawkins

There was an eerie silence as I walked down the creepy corridor. The only noises heard were distant cries and screams. I walked down the corridor, checking behind me every five seconds. I kept hearing noises but by the time I had realised, they went away. I turned a corner and found myself in a dusty room. I scanned the room for an exit, but all I found was an old baby carrier rocking a baby to sleep. Except... there was no baby! Just a note saying 'I am Sady Hawkins, the ghost who walks these halls. Leave my home...'.

Molly-Mae Priest (10)
St Margaret's At Hasbury CE Primary School, Hasbury

The Box On The Beach

One summer afternoon I took my best friend Otis for a walk. Otis liked to explore and the beach was his favourite place to go. This time, however, Otis stopped and began to dig. The sand was flying in the air.

"Otis, what have you found?"

Woof! I took a look down the hole. I could see an old wooden box with the letters 'E' and 'Z' on top. Inside the box there was a compass and a map! We followed the map to its destination. It was End Zone, a new land of technology...

Zachary Joe Eeles (9)

St Margaret's At Hasbury CE Primary School, Hasbury

Bank Madness

I got a call because someone had robbed the bank! I jumped into my car and rushed to the building. There was a police officer outside. He said, "There are some clues inside, try and find out who it was!"

Without hesitation, I ran into the building. When I got into the building I scanned the place for any clues. I saw a black object on the floor. I went to look at it. It was a black glove! I picked it up and put it in my pocket... The robber has now been caught. He's in jail.

Phoebe Whitehouse (10)

St Margaret's At Hasbury CE Primary School, Hasbury

The Lonely Shipwrecked Girl

I stared out of the delicate palace window staring at the sea desperately. My eyes watching, my ears pricked, my mind fizzing with excitement, but as normal, nothing. Pheobe gave a sad sigh, gazing out of the window impatiently and then turned, heartbroken, and scampered off. Morning came and sunlight flooded into the palace. Pheobe rushed to the window and noticed a tiny blur in the sea. Was it a ship heading towards her island? It was! People hurried out of it. Excitedly, she realised it was her lost parents! Pheobe ran, embracing them, and knew she'd never let go.

Chloe Godman (8)

St Mark's CE Primary School, Tunbridge Wells

Bad Unicorn

The bad unicorn stole everybody's magic in the dead of night! The magic turned bad. In the morning every unicorn screamed. Nobody knew her. Some unicorns called her spooky. When they were sleeping, the unicorns with the best powers would be hypnotised as her servants! At sunset, she said her catchphrase, "Being bad is the best!" Down in her caverns in the forest of death, she stared at all the magic she had collected. Just five more and she would have every unicorn in Dreamland! She would take all their magic powers and unleash the ultimate bad power...

Emma Lukowska (8)
St Mark's CE Primary School, Tunbridge Wells

Jurassic Park Adventure!

"Hello, I'm Steve. Nice to meet you!"

"What are you doing here? You should be in Minecraft!"

"What are you doing here, you should be in Roblox?"

"No I shouldn't!"

"Oh."

This went on for several hours, after Owen came back to Jurassic Park. I, Addy, decided to update Minecraft so Steve could be offline and get out of my face, so I did. It didn't turn out how I wanted. I lost connection so I had to leave! Owen came up to me somehow and gave me Robux, so I bought new clothes!

Asya Celik (8)

St Mark's CE Primary School, Tunbridge Wells

Haunted House

Creak! Crack! Creak! Crack! Went the creaking door on that very haunted night where the spirits came back alive. All terror arrived! While everyone was making costumes and carving pumpkins, one little boy had entered, not knowing all of his nightmares were about to hunt him down. As the boy walked in, a ghostly voice echoed around the hall. "Once you're in, you won't come out!" With one step, the dusty door slammed and he was locked in! He cried for help but no one could hear him. He was trapped forever. This wasn't a dream!

Idthel Kaniyara (9)
St Mark's CE Primary School, Tunbridge Wells

The Hidden Door

The wind was howling one night. A small girl Zarah was wandering in the wild woods. Little did she know, something lived there behind a secret door. What was it? What colour skin did it have? Where was the door? Suddenly, Zarah heard a horrifying noise. When she looked back, there was a hard brick wall! She had absolutely no escape now. There was that terrifying monstrosity of a noise again! It grew louder. She saw a red button and pushed it! The secret door had been opened. "It's a hairy, scary monster!" Zarah was never seen again...

Brooke Simmons (10)

St Mark's CE Primary School, Tunbridge Wells

Presumed Lost

I live with my mother and usually my brother Bertie but he's off fighting in the war. He is my best friend but I think he's gone. Right now I'm standing outside Bertie's empty bedroom. I miss him. Hot tears trickle down my cheeks but I quickly wipe them away. Suddenly I hear a siren and Mother screaming, "Run to the bomb shelter!"
In the cramped, dark shelter someone touches my shoulders. I turn and stitched to his uniform is the name Bertie. My brother's not lost, he's safe and we are a proper family again!

Rosie Jane Layberry (10)
St Mark's CE Primary School, Tunbridge Wells

Haunted House

One day two teenagers girls went into an abandoned house. They went to explore and they found a doll and all they did was laugh at it. Then it came to life like it was being controlled! They screamed and bumped into a skeleton. They screamed even more and their screams echoed all around the house. When it reached the end of the haunted house, ghosts came! They possessed everything except them! When they got into a different room, they found out it was a library! They were reading and then a secret passage appeared... They never returned!

Aimee Kirkness King (10)
St Mark's CE Primary School, Tunbridge Wells

Mystery Video Game

Two children, Bella and Jacob, had two lives only in a video game that sucked them in. A piece of paper read 'Level One: Run'. Behind them they saw lava! "Run!" Bella yelled. They ran so fast that in one minute they saw the place they were meant to reach but it was too far to get to it in time. John picked Bella up and threw her to safety but John had lost a life!

The paper read 'Last level: School. Answer this to leave. In French, how do you say game?'.

Bella thought. "Is it jeu?" They won!

Harley Squires (10)
St Mark's CE Primary School, Tunbridge Wells

Red Ninja Vs Moon Knight

One day a battle was causing chaos all over Explosive Island. The leader, Red Ninja, was battling Moon Knight. Moon Knight whacked his staff at Red Ninja, *kapow!* Red Ninja threw one of his weapons at Moon Knight as he replied, "This is too boring!"

Moon Knight left. The whole of Explosive Island had an idea. The plan was ready! Moon Knight returned the next day. He saw Red Ninja, or so he thought. When he threw his staff at Red Ninja, it went through as if it was cardboard! It was! As a cage trapped him, he was banished...

Dylan Squires (7)

St Mark's CE Primary School, Tunbridge Wells

Time Travel Phone Booth

It was a normal day. Noah was walking home from school when suddenly a phone booth appeared. Noah went in and dialled a number but it didn't ring. Instead, it started spinning round and round! It stopped spinning. Noah made a quick exit. Everything looked the same. Nothing was different. The trees were the same and the river too! He shrugged it off and carried walking down the street but then he realised the street wasn't the same. It was dark and everybody was wearing different clothes! He realised he was in the Victorian era...

Alfie Wright (10)

St Mark's CE Primary School, Tunbridge Wells

The Warren

In the year 3232 there were two friends, Jack and Joe. The friends were twelve. In a town of death, the house was sheltered to protect them. They had a pistol. There was a zombie apocalypse. It was terror and horror. They were scared because no one was there to protect them. Zombies were coming! As quick as a flash, they fired their guns and found a house and bolted the door! They were firing their guns. *Pew! Pew! Pew!* Finally, there were no more zombies left! They survived the apocalypse. "Yay!" they shouted.

Tyler Sturmer (9)
St Mark's CE Primary School, Tunbridge Wells

The Stray Dog

Once in a small and old orphanage lived a woman who ran the orphanage. She had twenty-four children there. One of the children was called Bella and she found something mysterious out on the street. She found a stray dog! It was lying down on the ground. When Bella went back to the orphanage, she found some papers inside the woman's desk with the owner's details. She found out that the owner was scared of dogs! Bella found a way to get the owner to like dogs again. Bella threw a party to make the owner like dogs again!

Nyah Leek (8)
St Mark's CE Primary School, Tunbridge Wells

The Magical Starfish

On a mysterious, sandy beach called Paradise Island lived a sea creature. A beautiful mermaid with a shimmering purple and pink fin named Pearl. Pearl lived in a giant clamshell but she loved to explore in the ocean. With her best friends, Sally the seahorse and Dolly the dolphin, they hunted to find rare magical starfish.

Years and years went by but not a glimmer of hope. Until one day. Deep down in the coral they found the sparkly starfish! It was trapped so Pearl let it free. Could this be the rare, magical starfish?

Pixie Lewis (8)

St Mark's CE Primary School, Tunbridge Wells

The Five Missing Gold Rings

One cold stormy night, a king was at the wedding of his son, Prince Charming. He was getting married to Cinderella, the daughter of the evil stepmother. The day of the wedding, his five golden rings were stolen by one of the guests! The king said to his son, "The rings have been stolen!" They called Detective Aimee. She found footprints leading to the basement. They found Harry in the basement with the rings! The detective grabbed Harry and took him to give the rings back. Then they took him to jail!

Aimee Leigh Watson (11)

St Mark's CE Primary School, Tunbridge Wells

Mind Games

Walking through the beaming light portal, flashes of yellow and blue raced past me until there I was, shaking with fear in a forest. Not just any forest, it was dark. The leaves on the trees were purple and there was a cool breeze rushing through the air, whistling through the broad gaps in between the trees. I took a step, brushing past the unusual leaves. The second I touched them, colours were fading and swirls of black and white hurried past me! Once my eyes adjusted to the dark, I realised it was just a dream!

Valentina Stopps (11)

St Mark's CE Primary School, Tunbridge Wells

The Save Of Majesty Nature!

One day a lady was walking in a park in New York. This was not a normal lady. She was Majesty Nature, a superhero. Suddenly she heard a sound coming out of the bush. She took a look and there was a hurt puppy! She turned into her superhero form and picked it up. "Hey, little pup!" Majesty Nature exclaimed.

The puppy gave a tiny, painful yelp. She ran over to the trees and hid, holding the puppy. The lady got her powers ready and healed the wound! The puppy was happy. Then the lady turned back and walked away.

Emily Lewis (9)
St Mark's CE Primary School, Tunbridge Wells

Gateway To A Weird World

I hit the ground with a thud and immediately knew something was wrong. Suddenly I realised I was on the ceiling! I looked up at the floor and then realised I could not go outside because if I did, I would have an eternal fall. Unexpectedly, the ground shook and I found myself in the pursuit of a ginormous T-rex! I ran as fast as my legs could carry me and I got to the next room. Gasping for breath, I stopped, only to find the T-rex gaining on me! I ran into the hall, sprinted down and jumped outside...

Alfie Abrosimoff Jubb (10)

St Mark's CE Primary School, Tunbridge Wells

Specimen

I began to slowly wake up. Everything felt heavy and sore. I couldn't distinguish numbness from pain. Slowly, a blinding light approached. A strange creature with sharp teeth and a discoloured boneless face came into view! Thoughts of fear danced around in my mind. "Don't worry, human. You'll be returned after a brief interlude."
They forced me to drink a bubbling blue liquid which burned my throat! Everything blurred... I woke up in bed. It was just a dream! I lifted my hands to rub my eyes but instead of fingers, they had been replaced by rubbery tentacles!

Isabella Patricia Patterson (11)

Tudor Grange Samworth Academy, Leicester

The Never-Ageing Portal

I crept into the mysterious portal, trying to find the missing children. I didn't know what was coming for me. When my eyes adjusted, I saw them. They didn't alter a bit! Some were flying in UFOs! I went to touch them. They were holograms! I gasped in awe. I wanted to leave. My feet lifted into the atmosphere! An ice-cold shiver spread down my spine. A whirling noise came from behind me. The portal was closing! The children made intense eye contact with me. They surrounded me! I'd come to save them and now I needed saving myself! "Help!"

Charlotte Garratt (10)

Tudor Grange Samworth Academy, Leicester

The Earth Warrior

In a mysterious world which was alive, there was a secret organisation building monstrous robots. One day, they attacked, leaving the world in despair! They evolved arms and legs, making them stronger than any living being! However, there was one human who wanted to fight back. He trained day and night. He invented an enhancing serum that gave him super strength! One by one, he took out the robots until he finally reached the robot control centre! He destroyed it, and the evil mechanical genius who had planned to take over the world. The Earth was saved!

Leo Crawford (10)

Tudor Grange Samworth Academy, Leicester

My Worst Nightmare

I was home. I was alone. Watching TV, my eyelids were slowly shutting. *Bang!* A book fell off the shelf. I was about to pick it up when... Powercut! Well, that's what I thought. Creeping through the house, I checked the power box. It was gone! Swiftly I ran to the door. It was locked! Looking for the keys with fear coursing through my veins, I couldn't catch a breath because... It caught me! At 3am, my parents came back. My mum suddenly screamed as a mysterious figure dashed past the dingy hallway... Now it had caught all of us!

Thomas Piotr Stepien (10)

Tudor Grange Samworth Academy, Leicester

Six Dead, One Alive

I knew this wasn't a good idea. We were strolling through the woods. I knew something wasn't right. All of a sudden, we came across a small cottage. When I stepped inside, there was nothing! Only an intermittent sound piercing my ears. When I walked on the floorboards, I noticed that one of them was loose. Then it snapped! We all fell down a black hole and only three of us made it! There was a creature chasing us! It caught up. It murdered my friends! Their shrill screams will haunt me forever. I'm the only one here now...

Ivana Golic (11)
Tudor Grange Samworth Academy, Leicester

Shape-Shifters

Stretching and yawning, I lumbered down the stairs in my school uniform. Everything seemed normal. I opened the door. All I could see was a rainbow tunnel! I decided to go and explore. I couldn't believe it. I was in a different place. Everyone around me was turning into different things! A man turned into a monkey. A woman turned into a fox. Everyone was shape-shifting! I wanted to get home before it happened to me! I ran back to my house. Passing the hallway mirror, I saw a strange hog. It wasn't a hog. It was me...

Ella Rudkin (11)

Tudor Grange Samworth Academy, Leicester

Shooting Toys!

I saw a black hole. I scrutinised it, wondering where it led. I decided to investigate. Suddenly, out came a toy! I picked it up. His head twisted all the way around. Many toys were shooting out of the hole! *I ought to run away. Why were they here? Who sent them?* The ground was shaking! What was happening? Out came thousands of toys. I felt dizzy. Then... I dropped to the floor! My brain felt like it was shrinking. My body felt light. I looked at my hands... They were plastic! I had become a toy!

Kaisha Nugent (10)
Tudor Grange Samworth Academy, Leicester

The Man

I entered the spine-chilling forest. A rush of mild wind coursed past me. I scanned my surroundings to check where it was coming from. Among the trees was a luminous light! I trudged across the pathway and peered through the trunks of the trees. I saw an old man with a boneless face! He had a hat and red eyes. Thoughts of fear danced around my mind. I tried to back away from the creature but suddenly, a twig snapped! He turned with a jerk and glared at me. My eyes widened. That was the last night I saw.

Ruby Tebbutt (11)
Tudor Grange Samworth Academy, Leicester

The Kidnapped Girl

When I awoke in handcuffs I looked around panicking. The only light source was the timer. A bomb! Three minutes! I struggled until I felt a heavy ball. Grabbing it, I threw it at the ticking timer! That's when dark smoke came rushing out, followed by a key. Unlocking the handcuffs, I left the room. A new room appeared! I longed for the outside world. How could I escape? The metal door was boiling hot but the floor was ice-cold! "Help me..." were the words I said. *Goodbye, world.*

Fia Fragnoli (10)

Tudor Grange Samworth Academy, Leicester

The Day I Became Part Of The Earth

As I entered the dark woods, I felt a rush of icy air sweep past me. The further I walked, the colder it got. Suddenly I saw it! A mysterious figure. *Blink.* It was closer. Without warning, I felt bony fingers grabbing at my arm but I turned to see no one behind me. What was happening? Suddenly strong arms dragged at my ankles, pulling me into the dirt! I clawed at roots and branches to no avail. I became part of the earth. At that moment, I knew that I would never again see the light of day.

Shaan Hussain (10)

Tudor Grange Samworth Academy, Leicester

The World Of Myths And Legends

It was yesterday when it happened. My mum bought it from the old shop in town that no one went to. A board game called unicorns and dragons. We played it. I won the first round. However, the real prize was being transported to a world of myths and legends!

I woke up. A unicorn was tickling me. I looked up and dragons encircled me! What made me scared was the high castle. I didn't know who lived there and I didn't want to! I wanted to go home. *Is there a way back?*

Peace Omorogieva (10)

Tudor Grange Samworth Academy, Leicester

Psychic?

I needed to get changed. When I opened the wardrobe door, what looked like a black hole engulfed me! When my eyes adjusted, I saw nothing but black! Suddenly, a figure appeared who I recognised. A boy that had gone missing! I saw him inside a deep well. He was unconscious! I blinked and I was back in my bedroom. I had to save him! I called the fire department. I raced to the scene and saw the police pulling out a pale body from the hole. My vision saved his life! Was I psychic?

Divine Mushinga (10)
Tudor Grange Samworth Academy, Leicester

Memories

My wardrobe was vibrating. Confused, I opened the doors to see a light. Reaching my arm out, I was sucked in! Floating in a haze, suddenly clear of my past, it flashed in front of me. A certain memory caught my attention! A baby in a pram. Me. A man was protecting me from a thief! I had a vague memory of my father. Could that be him? He had been killed in a knife attack. Now I knew the truth! I reached out to touch, but the image disintegrated... I was back in bed.

Arjunpal Singh (10)
Tudor Grange Samworth Academy, Leicester

A Brave Warrior

It lurks, waiting in the shadows for an unlucky victim to pass. Then it pounces, forcing its razor-sharp canines into the poor soul's heart. Eventually it lets go, after taking the victim's life. This beast lives at the bottom of Loch Ness and terrified tourists stay away.

News spread far and wide but only one man plucked up the courage to teach this beast a lesson - a Danish man called Whitgils. The instant Whitgils arrived, the beast emerged! Whitgils grabbed the terror's arms. It tried to flee but it couldn't! In the end, its arms were ripped off.

Freya Hawley (8)
Yattendon School, Horley

The Super Adventure

Once there was a ninja called Superdoor. His master said that there was a mission. When he went there, he got kidnapped! When he woke up, he saw he was inside a spaceship that was going to explode in two minutes! He didn't know what to do. He was thinking so much. Then he had five seconds. The spaceship exploded! He remembered he could fly so he flew home! It took him one day. When he got home, his brothers said, "Welcome back!"

Superdoor went to sleep. When he woke up, he felt good. He said, "What an adventure!"

Affan Saymum (8)
Yattendon School, Horley

The Mystery Of Azel-Wick...

I was running through the haunted corridors of Azel-Wick Manor. The door suddenly creaked open! I ran and ran and ran as fast as my legs could go. In a heart-stopping moment, something tapped me on the shoulder! I turned around anxiously, scared of what could be behind me. I saw a shadow and before I could open my eyes, it disappeared into the darkness! Hearing something behind me, I carefully turned round. A strange disfigurement stood in front of me...

She was never to be seen again. The police searched but they said she was gone.

Kirsty JJ Writer (10)

Yattendon School, Horley

Time Travel

It was a completely normal day in my lab. Then I heard an ear-ringing bash! I turned around. It was the time travel portal. It had opened and was sucking all my things in, including me! When I finally opened my eyes, I wasn't in my lab anymore. Everything was super high-tech and that's when I realised I was in the year 5000! It was an outstanding place with monumental buildings. That's when I saw it. It looked minuscule at first but then it got larger... Suddenly, I woke up in a puddle of sweat. It was all a dream!

Isabella Valentina Carvajal Chacin (10)
Yattendon School, Horley

Super Wing And The Monster

One upon a time there was a city called Cobla. There was a bad thing that happened. A monster appeared! Suddenly a hero came. His name was Super Wing. He hit the monster and he was knocked out! Then Super Wing shot lasers at him. It did nothing! "Oh no," he said. "We're doomed!" Then Super Wing thought of a plan. He needed back-up. He called his team and they destroyed the monster. Then in a flash, the monster was gone forever! Since then, nobody has ever seen him since. Everybody was happy again. It was Super Wing City!

Mohammad Islam (7)

Yattendon School, Horley

Superhero School For Boys

I strolled into a mysterious learning environment. *What shall I do?* It wasn't my classroom and it wasn't my classmates! My teachers looked like aliens! My classroom looked like a battlefield and my classmates looked like superheroes. *Shall I run away, go home or learn the way of the superheroes?* I ran down the road and then realised that everyone had superpowers! Maybe I had superpowers too? Yes, I did! What should I use them for? Where should I go? I made up my mind. I was going to go to superhero school...

Lucas Griffin (8)
Yattendon School, Horley

Secret Door

I stepped through the dark, dingy hallway and at the far end was a secret door. I stepped into the secret door, not knowing what I would find. Inside was a magical, wonderful world hidden beneath the door! I gasped in awe at the amazing animals, each glowing in a different light - pinks, greens, blues and yellows. Each pathway led to a different creature, some big and some as small as ants! This only meant one thing... Every door you open in life leads to different paths. Choose wisely. It could lead to magical things!

Ruby Westwood (8)
Yattendon School, Horley

A Sad Unicorn Called Mal

One day a door came to my room. I stepped through it to see a colourful world! In the corner of my eye, I spotted a sad-looking unicorn. As quick as a flash, I darted to it. I asked, "What's wrong?" She said she had lost her parents and had been looking for them for weeks! She looked cold and hungry so I gave her some food I had in my bag. I helped her look for her parents. We found them! I didn't want to leave but I did. I felt very happy and very very proud!

Phoebe May Bellinger (8)
Yattendon School, Horley

Magic Is In The Air

I slowly put my hand out without opening my eyes and felt soft fur, as soft as snow. I opened one eye. I opened the other eye. I couldn't believe it! Right in front of me was a mythical, magical unicorn! I slowly lifted my feet and without thinking, jumped onto the unicorn's back. We rode into the sunset.

Olivia Harding (9)

Yattendon School, Horley

It's Me...

Dead. The knife embedded deep in his back. Sherlock looked around for clues. "Hmm, I see the problem. I'll get my fingerprint detector!" He ran out of the office. No one noticed Henry crouching under the table. When Sherlock came back, he looked at the fingerprints. "Ah! They belong to Henry, but where is he?"

"Achoo!" Henry accidentally sneezed.

"Aha, gotcha!" Sherlock shouted, grabbing Henry's hands and holding them behind his back.

"Ugh, you got me!" Henry grunted.

"I knew it was you!" Sherlock said.

"But I bet you didn't know that I'll get you and kill you, muahaha..."

Maisie Elizabeth Thompson (10)

Yealand CE Primary School, Yealand Redmayne

The Churching Hour

The coffin was buried. It was done. We walked back inside mournfully, listening to the priest talk. Then the pews gave way. The people vanished! The door locked and the altar flipped upside-down, revealing a door! I was mortified, frozen stiff with horror. The door creaked open and zombies, vampires and soul-suckers came swarming out! So did the Grim Reaper and many ghosts! They haunted the deserted church, gathering, moving in for the kill. I was dragged through the door to a dungeon. I was left there to rot but then a soul-sucker took me into a blank, eternal void...

James Proctor (11)
Yealand CE Primary School, Yealand Redmayne

Roblox Adventure

I was playing Roblox and suddenly I got sucked in!
Something said, "Complete four simulators in a
week!"
I started by playing a simulator about boxing.
People kept hitting me but I completed that in a
day! Then the following one was with a lightsaber.
I got really good and completed it in no time. The
next simulator was about getting good pets, it was
easy! I completed it in an hour. The following one
was about unboxing hats. I got the best hat but it
took ages!
Then the speaker said, "You're stuck, lost in the
game. You failed..."

Luke Zak Robinson (10)
Yealand CE Primary School, Yealand Redmayne

The Way To Wi-Fi

Darkness, then light. I was in a room filled with obstacles. Then a booming voice said, "If you want to go on the Internet ever again, you will complete this course in under five minutes! Three, two, one, go!"
I set off. First, the monkey bars. My arms had no energy and I still had ten more to go! Over the lake infested with crocodiles...Through laser beams! Then a fifty-metre sprint. Thirty seconds left... Would I make it? My legs pumped and then I made it! I was free to go back on the amazing, incredible, fantastic Internet!

Ellie Proctor (11)
Yealand CE Primary School, Yealand Redmayne

The Graveyard Mystery

Billy and Grace had stayed up late to go adventuring in the graveyard. It was 3am. They set off. Five minutes into the journey, there was a rattle in the trees! They turned around and there was nothing there... Then there it was again! This time there was a pair of red eyes staring at them! They thought it was just a bat, so they carried on. Another three minutes later, a gravestone fell! This time they got scared. Then another fell down and another and another! They were spooked out. They didn't know what to say...

Sebastian Bould (10)

Yealand CE Primary School, Yealand Redmayne

Zombie Land

I accidentally died. I was put in the coffin. It was a magical portal which teleported me to a place that I called Zombie Land because all you can see in the streets are zombies! Suddenly, when I arrived there I was chased by a zombified zombie! I ran past a shop so I went in circles and went into the shop and celebrated. I found a helicopter! I flew it to an abandoned place and was chased by ten zombies! I ran around and suddenly found a portal. I ran into it...

Max Ideson (10)
Yealand CE Primary School, Yealand Redmayne

YOUNG WRITERS INFORMATION

We hope you have enjoyed reading this book – and that you will continue to in the coming years.

If you're a young writer who enjoys reading and creative writing, or the parent of an enthusiastic poet or story writer, do visit our website **www.youngwriters.co.uk**. Here you will find free competitions, workshops and games, as well as recommended reads, a poetry glossary and our blog. There's lots to keep budding writers motivated to write!

If you would like to order further copies of this book, or any of our other titles, then please give us a call or order via your online account.

Young Writers
Remus House
Coltsfoot Drive
Peterborough
PE2 9BF
(01733) 890066
info@youngwriters.co.uk

Join in the conversation!
Tips, news, giveaways and much more!

f YoungWritersUK   **🐦** @YoungWritersCW

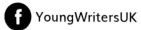